THE MOUSE ON WALL STREET

Leonard Wibberley

The Mouse On Wall Street
Copyright © 1969, 1997 by Leonard Wibberley

New Paperback Edition Published by
The Estate of the Late Leonard Wibberley
leonardwibberleybooks@gmail.com

http://leonardwibberley.wix.com/author

Sign up for our monthly newsletter to receive columns written by Leonard Wibberley that were syndicated by newspapers nationally over his lifetime. You will also receive news of the upcoming releases of the ebook and paperback editions of his many novels.

http://bit.ly/LeonardNews

Cover Art Stock Photos by Dreamstime & Canstockphoto

All rights reserved.
No part of this publication may be reproduced or transmitted in any form or by any means, electronic or mechanical, including photocopy, recording, or any information storage and retrieval system, without permission in writing from the publisher.

ISBN-13: 978-1518741630
ISBN-10: 1518741630

CHAPTER I

The world was, as usual, out of sorts. To be sure, no crisis greater than normal (and it was a sign of the times that there was a certain normalcy about crises) loomed on the political or military fronts of Europe or Asia. Negotiations for peace between the United States and Northern Afghanistan were entering the third year with hope held out that a place would shortly be agreed between the two sides at which to meet to start considering an agenda for the talks. At home in the United States groups of Polish-American students were rioting on college campuses and had shut down the University of Chicago, demanding that the contribution of the Polish people to American history be emphasized in the college curriculum. They were opposed by groups of Russian-American students, who insisted that the Poles wished only to defame the Russian nation.

Chinese-American students had burned down four libraries in the interest of academic freedom and to protest that that part played by Chinese laborers in laying the first continental railroad line was utterly ignored in American textbooks.

In Eastern Europe the tanks of a hugely expanded Soviet Army were restoring the People's Democracies in Rumania and Hungary, rumbling through the streets of cities with their own particular brand of liberty or death. The taxi drivers of Milan were on strike to protest the engagement of Karl Schmidt, a German, to sing the title role in a production of Otello at La Scala.

These routine crises did not disturb the Count of Mountjoy, seated in his study in the castle of the Duchy of Grand Fenwick, of which nation he was Prime Minister. It was early morning and the Count, silver-haired, aristocratic in bearing as well as in name, seemed scarcely a day older than he had been fourteen years previously when he had saved the world from atomic destruction by the seizure of the Q-bomb, which still rested on its straw-padded pedestal in the dungeon of the castle.

What did concern the Count was the inefficiency of the postman on whom the Duchy depended for its overseas mail service. Letters for the Duchy, which shared a border of a quarter of a mile in extent with France, its ancient enemy, were brought by a French bus driver by the name of Salat, who was of a moody disposition. If he felt, after reading his morning paper, that his country had been insulted or taken advantage of, he avenged his national honor by discontinuing the mail service to Grand Fenwick. Mail might lie in the postbox on the Duchy's borders for two or three days until the bus driver felt sufficiently mollified to pick it up. And during that interval, of course, he would refuse to deliver letters from abroad—sometimes letters of official concern addressed to the Count of

Mountjoy or to the sovereign lady of the Duchy, Her Grace Gloriana XII.

This greatly irritated the Count, who had many times written to the Ministry of Foreign Affairs in France on the matter only to be met with the bland and meaningless phrases of diplomacy which he often employed himself.

So, that morning in September, while the world was concerned with riot and military threat, the balance of trade and the price of gold, the Count of Mountjoy awaited with some anxiety news of whether his copy of the *Times* of London had been delivered or whether Salat had once more decided to boycott Grand Fenwick for a day or two.

However, on such a glorious morning with the chirping of birds melodious and liquid, coming to him from the nearby Forest of Grand Fenwick, with the fields and vineyards bathed in the generous sunlight of autumn, it was impossible for Mountjoy to be irritated for long. From a road below skirting the castle, the Count heard the rumbling of iron-rimmed cartwheels and the clumping of heavy hoofs on the drawbridge as yet another wagon entered the castle courtyard laden with the small black grapes from which are produced that wine coveted by the connoisseurs of the world—Pinot Grand Fenwick. The grape harvest had been excellent. The grapes were small, firm, and high in sugar content. No more than five thousand bottles would result from the harvest and these would command tremendous prices in the world market. The wool clip had been excellent too, and the fleeces of Grand Fenwick, like the wine of

Grand Fenwick, commanded a high price abroad. White-faced mountain sheep provided those fleeces which when carefully washed in the icy streams of the Duchy produced a wool with a delicate shade of cream highly esteemed by the mills of England.

Wine and wool were between them the total national resources of Grand Fenwick, which, being only five miles long and three miles broad in its greatest extent, supported but five thousand souls. The nation, one of the smallest sovereign states in the world, was unique in many respects, not least among them the fact that it had balanced its budget for the past five hundred years and its currency was absolutely sound. Not for Grand Fenwick the spiral of wages and prices, the worries over inflation and deflation and the anxieties of combating an adverse balance of trade. The finance and commerce of the Duchy were in precise balance. Exports and imports between them formed a partnership which made impossible any dangerous rise of either prices or wages, and the Grand Fenwick pound, together with the Swiss franc, was pronounced by men of finance the soundest of the world's currencies.

Founded by Sir Roger Fenwick in 1475 (Old Style), there had been but one year that Grand Fenwick had had to go abroad for funds to balance its budget, and support its people. That year, 1954, the problem had been solved by declaring war on the United States of America. Under the terms of the peace treaty which resulted from the victory of Grand Fenwick, the Duchy had been given the right to sell its wine in the United States without tariff or impost and also to manufacture in the United States and sell there a chewing gum with the unique flavor of its famous wine, Pinot Grand Fenwick. The right to make and sell the Pinot gum had been given under the contract to an American manufacturer on condition of receiving a royalty on profits and a holding of 45 percent of the common stock of the manufacturing company. There were no profits and there were no royalties, but royalties were not missed. Wine and wool provided all the income the Duchy needed.

"God has always had us in his special care," mused the Count, viewing the pleasant landscape about from his window. "We have lived with the esteem of the world, with no ambitions upon the territories of our neighbors, with respect for the rights of others, supporting ourselves by our labor and by the fruits of the soil. We are enemies of none and bear ill will toward none." His eye strayed to where the white and winding road disappeared into the Gap of Pinot toward the border and he added, "Except, of course, the damnable French."

At that moment he caught sight of a figure on a bicycle coming up the road toward the castle. From the height of his study window, the figure appeared little bigger than a beetle, but he knew immediately that this was Will Creman, one of the border guards, now relieved of duty and bringing, he trusted, the morning mail, including a copy of the *Times* which would be no more than three days old.

Will came on fast, passing a cart lumbering up the road with its load of grapes. Mountjoy was probably the only statesman in the world who could sense a crisis in the speed of a man on a bicycle and he sensed one now. Will did not, passing the cart, slow down for a word with the carter, who waved his whip at him. He sped on, scattered a company of geese nibbling grass and dandelion leaves by the roadside, and wheeled over the drawbridge into the courtyard at a brisk pace.

"Probably an airmail letter," said Mountjoy. "Which means a letter from America. Nobody else uses air mail."

Sure enough, when, fifteen minutes later, Will presented himself at the door of the Count's study, he had an airmail letter from America in his hand.

"From New York," said Will, as if he were saying "From Venus" or "From Saturn." And he added, "It was in America only four days ago. And now it's here in Grand Fenwick. Makes you sort of excited to think of it."

"Would you like to go to New York?" asked the Count.

"I were there fifteen years back come Michelmas," said Will. "When we took the city. Met a girl called Rosie. Only saw her for three minutes. Real American girl. Funny how you remember something like that. Could I have the stamps?"

"You're collecting them?" asked the Count.

Will blushed. "No, my lord," he said. "It's because of Rosie. Sort of makes me feel…well … a little more in touch with her. Having something from her country… See?"

"Yes," said Mountjoy, "I do see," and he carefully tore the stamps from the letter and gave them to Will.

When Will had gone the Count remained for a moment looking

at the closed door. Then he sighed, opened the letter, throwing the envelope on the floor as was his custom, and glanced at the letterhead. The name, Bickster and Company, of Pacific Grove, New Jersey, seemed vaguely familiar, though he could not immediately place it. He turned to the contents, which read:

The Honorable Count of Mountjoy,
Prime Minister to Her Grace Gloriana XII The Castle,
Grand Fenwick

Dear Sir:
We are delighted to inform you that this year, for the first time, there has been a great and welcome increase in the sales of our product due in part to a change in the social habits of the consuming public and in part, we believe, to our adroit exploitation of this changing situation.

At this point the Count lowered the letter with a grimace. "'Social habits of the consuming public,' " he repeated aloud. "What in God's name do they mean by that? What a frightful way to think of people. 'Consuming public.' Like boa constrictors swallowing everything that is put in front of them." Having relieved his feelings in some degree by this outburst, the Count continued reading the letter:

You are undoubtedly aware of the recent report of the Surgeon

General of the United States detailing the relationship between cigarette smoking and lung cancer as well as cancer of the bladder, restriction and hardening of the kidneys…

"Damn," said the Count of Mountjoy. "What is it about Americans that they can make anatomical details sound so revolting? 'Cancer of the bladder.' I've managed to live for over three quarters of a century without even acknowledging the existence of my bladder. These confounded people are in love with their insides."

He threw the letter to the floor, where it fell face down, and he gave it a kick with his foot as he went to the bellpull to tell his man to bring him a fresh pot of tea and some toasted Hovis bread and a pot of marmalade. In being kicked the letter flipped over, and out of the single sheet of a white paper a figure preceded by a dollar sign seemed to leap at him. He ignored it, thinking that this was probably some appeal for a donation to help forward the American antismoking crusade. Then, when his tea and his toast had been brought to him, the significance of the name on which he had been ruminating came to him. Bickster and Company, he now recalled, were the people in the United States who were authorized to manufacture and sell the Pinot Grand Fenwick chewing gum, which they had managed to do for so many years without bothering anybody in the Duchy!

Intrigued, the Count picked up the letter once more and, ignoring two further paragraphs detailing how Americans were switching from smoking to chewing, pounced on the last paragraph, which read:

> Total sales of Pinot Grand Fenwick chewing gum in the United States last year, after deduction of manufacturing, distributing, and advertising expenses, and also putting aside a reserve for further promotion and payment of state and federal taxes, showed a profit of $2,500,000. Under the terms of our agreement with yourselves, whereby you are to receive 40 percent of the profits, as that term is defined in Article 14, subsection a, of that agreement, you are to receive the sum of $1,000,000, which we have pleasure in sending to you through Lloyd's Bank in London...

The Count read no further. The hand in which he held the letter trembled slightly. A piece of toast, laden with marmalade, which he was conveying to his mouth remained in midair, arrested in mid-voyage, as the Count grasped the significance of what he had read.

"One million dollars," he cried. "One million dollars? It's an outrage. A confounded outrage, an unwarranted, planned, and dastardly invasion of our completely balanced economy. Those blackguards will ruin us."

CHAPTER II

It was the Count of Mountjoy's habit, when confronted with any crisis, to do nothing for a week but think about it and cautiously sound out others for their opinion on the matter. "Time," his father had often told him, "dissolves most crises. If you will examine the history of the world you will find that the greatest disasters have always resulted from hasty decisions. Furthermore, if God took seven days in which to make the world, you will never be blamed for taking three weeks to answer a letter. In that time you will often find the urgency has disappeared and no action at all is required on your part."

This advice the Count had always found sound, and confronted with the crisis of one million dollars in American currency about to be dumped into the Treasury of Grand Fenwick with not a project in sight on which it could be wasted, Mountjoy began to subtly investigate possible means of getting rid of the money without introducing it into the national economy to the nation's ruin.

He first questioned the Duchess, Gloriana XII ("as lovely a sovereign as ever Europe saw," in the Count's words), whether she would not like the whole of the ducal apartments in the castle completely redecorated in the most lavish style. She said she wouldn't.

"We've just finished a three-year redecoration plan, Bobo," she said. "If I see another paint pot or another ladder or roll of carpet, I think I'll scream. What have you got up your sleeve?" she asked, eying him closely, for she knew the Count well and knew that, while completely honorable, he was never without some hidden plan or project.

"Your Grace," said Mountjoy, "I have nothing which will remain hidden from you."

"But something you don't want to talk about right now?"

"Precisely, Your Grace," said Mountjoy. "There are times, as you know, when it is the duty of a servant to be silent, and this is such a time. Later, when the season is more fitting, every particle of what I have in my mind will be placed openly and frankly before you with such recommendations as I am able to offer."

"It is something to do with money, isn't it, Bobo?" asked Gloriana.

"Your Grace, it is something which involves far more than money. That much I can tell you while begging your indulgence in not pressing me further."

Gloriana nodded. She could never remember a time in her life when she had been able to refuse Mountjoy a request, for his language was always so courteous and he was always able to convince her that whatever he asked was entirely in her service. She turned to a related subject.

"The grape harvest, I think, will be the best in twenty years," she said. "Will it be possible to announce a slight tax reduction in January? I feel that we must leave more money in the hands of our people so that they can improve their own lives and living conditions. We take twelve percent of their income in taxes now. It is far too high."

"It is the lowest taxation rate anywhere in the Western world," replied Mountjoy.

"It is still too high," said Gloriana.

Mountjoy promised to see what he could do, but he was opposed to tax reduction, finding the present tax levy necessary to prevent inflation in the Duchy.

Unable to find a source of expenditure in Gloriana, Mountjoy sought out Tully Bascomb, Hereditary Grand Marshal of the Duchy and also Chief Forester, and consort to Her Grace. As consort his political position was nil, but two of his offices corresponded roughly to that of Minister of the Interior and Minister for War.

Of natural resources Grand Fenwick had but portions of three mountains and the Forest of Grand Fenwick, which comprised but five hundred acres, so forest was perhaps too large a word for it. All in Grand Fenwick, however, were enormously proud of these five hundred wooded acres and the post then of Chief Forester carried great eminence and respect in the Duchy. No budget expenditure on

Fenwick Forest was ever challenged, for between the people of the Duchy and the forest itself there was a sense of close and deep associations, as if the soul of the Duchy lived not in the castle but in the woods.

Pierce Bascomb, Tully's father and a man of great learning, had postulated that this particular feeling on the part of the people of Grand Fenwick was akin to the tree worship of pagans, which he pointed out survived in many parts of the world, as for instance in Wales, where the Great Oak of Carnarvon was held upright in the center of town by cement (when the oak fell, Wales would fall also), and in the proposal that the flag of the early American Revolutionaries should show a pine tree.

The elder Bascomb, bespectacled, tall and lean, was the author of two books on birds which had gained for him a world-wide reputation among ornithologists. His *Migratory Birds of Grand Fenwick* was widely hailed and his *Fenwickian Songbirds* was reckoned one of the better works of its kind published in Europe.

His son, Tully, had his father's tendency to scholarship. He was especially knowledgeable on the subject of trees and had read a paper before the Royal Society in London on the relationship between elm disease and soil bacteria which had gained him great respect in scientific circles. Tall like his father, muscular and inclined to be taciturn, he had traveled abroad more than any other in Grand Fenwick and was an astute student of politics, counseling the Duchess but never directly making a decision for her.

To Tully then the Count of Mountjoy went, finding him in the little hut in the forest which he used as an office. The Count said he was beginning some preparatory work on the budget for the coming year and that this would be a good time to spend rather heavily on the needs of the forest, hinting that considerable revenue was available from the wool and grape crop, for he wished for the time being to keep secret from all the news of the windfall from chewing gum.

But Tully disappointed him. All, it seemed, was well in the forest. No major expenditures were called for. A nice balance had been achieved between birds, insects and vegetation, and neither fertilizers nor insecticides were required for the health of the trees. Two thousand pounds, the equivalent of six thousand United States dollars, would be ample for the coming year.

"There will be no need for any great expense in the forest for some years," Tully said. "If we are going to have a budget surplus, why not remit some of the taxes? Many of our young people are prevented from attending universities abroad for lack of funds. Reduce the taxation of their parents and we will benefit as a nation from a rise in the educational level among our people."

"A reduction of taxation and an increase in the educational level are not necessarily beneficial," said Mountjoy testily. "I would remind you that very few people with a college degree turn to farming, and we are a nation which without farmers cannot exist. I dread to think what would happen to our sheep and our vineyards if the sons of yeomen such as Clemens, Whittakers and Asgood received degrees in philosophy, engineering and nuclear physics.

Higher learning, as it is called, of immense benefit in urban societies, can be disastrous in those with an agricultural base."

With that he left, having once more failed to find a method of ridding the Duchy of its unwanted windfall. There remained to him but one further resource, after which, should he fail here, he would have to inform the Duchess Gloriana at a meeting of her Privy Council both of the windfall itself and of his lack of success in formulating any plan for disposing of it.

His last hope was the eminent physicist, Dr. Kokintz, discoverer of the element quadium and therefore father of that most potent of all the atomic weapons, the quadium or Q-bomb. Kokintz had been born in Grand Fenwick, had been taken to the United States in his youth, and had returned to Grand Fenwick as a prisoner when the Duchy had captured the quadium bomb in its invasion of the United States, as is related elsewhere. He had remained voluntarily in the Duchy as the guardian of the Q-bomb and had found in the tiny country the freedom from pressures which he needed for his continuing research in physics. Scientific research being an increasingly expensive profession because of the high cost of the various tools used in investigating, Mountjoy had some confidence that Kokintz, offered a million dollars, would embrace the gift.

Dr. Kokintz had his laboratory in the Jerusalem Tower of Fenwick Castle. Here two airy apartments had been handed over to him, one for his paraphernalia and another, adjoining it and separated from it only by a sliding partition of golden oak, for a study and library. The great scientist shared with Pierce Bascomb a devotion to birds, and in the sunnier part of his laboratory, near the window, he had several cages of finches, goldfinches, canaries and little black and white Javanese ricebirds. Kokintz (when he had no noxious chemicals about) would often open up the cages and let his birds fly about and roost and twitter as they wished. He fed them with care and they were deeply attached to him. It was remarkable that when he entered the laboratory in the morning (or indeed at any time, for he visited his place of work whenever an idea occurred to him, day or night) the birds greeted him with a chorus of chirps and twitters like merry children seeing a favorite uncle at Christmastime.

Kokintz was no narrow scientist of the modern sort, with an eye on a Nobel Prize or at least a book which might become a lucrative college text. He belonged to the larger age of Darwin, having a love for and a curiosity about all forms of learning. He was preeminently a mathematician, so his approach to all subjects tended to be mathematical in the first instance. But he was capable both of imagination and of daringly original thought and had produced as a hobby a little book, beloved by the Senior Wranglers of Oxford, called *Mathematics for Fast Curves*—a sort of five-dimensional geometry in which, to the concepts of length, breadth and thickness, had been added the two dimensions of Time and Notime. The title was the publisher's. Kokintz had proposed "Calculating Principles for Nonrelated Absolutes."

A basic principle demonstrated by Kokintz in this little book was that in both eternity and infinity nothing moved or could move.

No change was possible in either of these states and no physical or chemical law of the finite and noneternal dimension could apply in them.

The book had been examined with interest by the Archbishop of Canterbury in the hope that a mathematical proof of the existence of Paradise would now be brought forward, but he bogged down hopelessly on page two. The Vatican, having examined the book carefully, accepted the recommendation of Cardinal Bruzelini of the censor's office, himself a noted theologian and mathematician, that the book be examined once every century.

"There is no heresy in it now for the reason that no one can understand it now," said the Cardinal. "But that may change later."

Kokintz was currently interested in one aspect of a field already widely investigated—the DNA molecule. By carefully cadging marbles from the boys of Grand Fenwick he had managed to construct for his amusement an excellent model of the DNA helix with some important variations from that offered by Nobel prize winners Crick and Watson. He was absorbed in the tautometric shift of hydrogen atoms in the sugars from the enol to keto configurations. And this in turn had led him into a new investigation of the "glue" or bonding force of hydrogen atoms and other atoms as well. This work, however, was now in abeyance, for Kokintz and the boys of Grand Fenwick had run out of marbles. This did not bother Kokintz. While waiting for more, he turned to other matters; for he took the large view that what one scientist did not discover, another certainly would, and science should not become a race to be the first with a discovery—an undignified scramble to publish before someone else published something on the same subject.

Kokintz was then, when the Count of Mountjoy called on him, busy with paper and pencil at a table in his study, the table itself overwhelmed by equipment of a formidable variety which had been pushed aside to make a little area to work at in the center.

"Evening," said the Count, sniffing the air a little. Then, removing a rack of test tubes from a comfortable leather chair, he sat down in it. Kokintz, busy with his paper, made no reply. "Bit stuffy in here," said Mountjoy. "I was wondering whether you wouldn't appreciate having the place air-conditioned. We could air-condition the whole castle, come to think of it. If the Americans are able to air-condition those enormous hotels of theirs, the castle should be quite easy."

"Why not open a window instead?" said Kokintz, peering up over his thick rimless glasses. "That window over there," he said, nodding his head in the direction of the window. "But be careful of the distillation unit."

"What are you doing?" demanded Mountjoy, moving to the window. "Making your own gin?"

Kokintz ignored this. He was aware that Mountjoy regarded all science with suspicion as being beneath the dignity of gentlemen and beyond the comprehension of peasants. Science had summoned into being, in the Count's opinion, a third social class which was learned, humorless and dangerous. He did not quite regard Kokintz in these terms, but there was no doubt at all that scientists as a class constituted a threat to the world, largely because they kept fiddling around with things that were much better left alone.

"Excuse me just a moment," said Kokintz. "I am at an important little point here. If I fumble, I have to do everything over again."

"Take your time," said Mountjoy. "I'll just look around a bit if you don't mind." He left the chair and started to poke about the study, examining vacuum bells and cabinets containing balances and cupboards full of glassware of the most unlikely shapes. When he got to the model of the DNA helix he recognized it immediately as a modern sort of Christmas tree. He uncovered a very stale sandwich in a corner with next to it a pad of paper on which were written some cabalistic symbols and the words *neon, argon* and *trace*. When he got back to his chair he had estimated the cost of replacing the total equipment in Kokintz's study and laboratory at a hundred thousand dollars. He felt a little more cheerful and was prepared to be grateful to science as a sort of rubbish dump for excess money.

"B flat, C sharp, and then D," said Kokintz. "The harmonic minor. Of course." He reached into the pocket of the old knitted cardigan he was wearing, took out what appeared to the Count to be a toy whistle and played three notes on it. "You see," he said, beaming. "It came out exactly as it should."

"What came out exactly as it should?" asked Mountjoy. "My little musical experiment," said Kokintz. "You are aware that all music is basically mathematics?"

"I'm not aware of anything of the sort," said Mountjoy. "I am aware that music is a form of communication which transcends language, is common to all humanity, and soothes the savage breast. If you have decided that it is all mathematics, spare me the explanation. I will not tolerate the conclusion that Mozart's *Magic Flute* is nothing but a mathematical formula."

"Oh no," said Kokintz. "But mathematics is the base. The art rests on a mathematical base—so many vibrations per second; so many beats to a bar. Birds have not found out about bars yet. When they make that discovery, they will be superb musicians because it is certainly the rhythm that makes music so appealing. The pitch I have discovered is secondary. All that birds have is pitch and an undeveloped sense of rhythm. If they could be taught to count—what melodies!"

"I suppose so," said Mountjoy. "But that isn't what I came here to talk to you about."

"You have a problem?" asked Kokintz, taking out his Oom-paul pipe and groping around for the tobacco pouch in his cardigan pocket.

"In a way," said Mountjoy. "In a way."

Kokintz waited and Mountjoy, seeking for a graceful way of introducing his subject, wished he knew more about the work of the great physicist. Since he didn't, he started with generalities.

"There are times, my dear Kokintz," he said, "when I have severe pangs of conscience concerning you and your work. I wonder whether I and the Duchy at large will not be held by posterity responsible for the projects which you were able to initiate and complete while living here. I wonder whether I and the Duchy will not be accused of unwittingly setting limits to what you are able to do, and that would be a heavy blot on our record in centuries to come."

"I will not leave," said Kokintz suspiciously. "I have as much right to stay here as you. Besides, you forget that it is part of our treaty that I must remain to see that the quadium bomb remains in good shape and is not interfered with by others."

"My dear fellow," said Mountjoy, "you completely mistake my meaning. Nobody in the Duchy wishes you to leave. Everybody would be highly distressed if you were to do so. No. No. I am concerned only with the limitations put on your work by our lack of financial support." He made a gesture which took in the whole of Kokintz's study.

"Little as I know about science," he said, "it seems to me that your equipment is all old-fashioned and that you need a completely new laboratory with electronic microscopes or whatever they are called, cloud chambers and cyclotrons and so on, so that you are not handicapped in devising and carrying out your various experiments. In looking around while you were busy with your little musical problem, as you call it, it occurred to me that perhaps you should be working on something of greater importance but could not do so for lack of facilities. I noted a great number of slips of paper lying around here and there, with scientific notations of one kind or another on them.

"Possibly they are of no importance. But possibly they and

others like them are the kind of information that should be stored in some kind of memory bank for the use of future generations."

To this Kokintz said nothing. He gathered that Mountjoy was in a generous mood and willing to spend some money. This was not unusual. The Count had erratic bursts of generosity usually around election time which were succeeded by equally erratic bursts of austerity. But he had never spoken before of memory banks. Kokintz didn't need a memory bank. Anything he wanted to remember he wrote on a slip of paper as the Count had seen and left it on one of his worktables. He always found it again, though sometimes it took a day or two. But in that time his memory and indeed his mind were stimulated by the information on all the other pieces of paper he had had to shuffle through first. And that was the way he liked to work.

"There are some excellent memory banks available now, I am told," said the Count. "Information from every part of the world and upon every subject can be fed into them and is instantly available to anyone who requires it anywhere. The saving is tremendous. Scientists are no longer in deep ignorance of each other's work. They can find out on the moment who is working on what and what has been achieved. The saving in time and work is enormous."

Kokintz shook his head. "You have a wrong view of scientists," he said. "Ninety percent of them are but very highly trained mechanics. They are not all busy originating research. The greater part are nothing but culture farmers raising generation after generation of bacteria in little dishes and counting the differing kinds. And it is necessary that this work be done—and not once but many,

many times. Of the original scientists in the world, however, there are scarcely a handful in any field, and you can be sure that they keep in close touch with each other regarding their work. Why, I have letters here from Intohaji in Japan and Bujorn in Finland gladly giving me details of their experiments and conclusions in a field in which we are all engaged."

"What field is that?" asked Mountjoy.

Kokintz sighed. "It is difficult to explain," he said. "When you were at school I am sure you often heard the formula 'acid plus base gives salt and water.' "

Mountjoy recalled the rule, drummed into his head by a chemistry professor who had always, at the corner of his mouth, a tiny white spot of saliva. He remembered the spot of saliva far more vividly than interactions of acids and alkalis and the chemistry of the multitude of carbons with which the whole world seemed to be infested, from lamp black to marsh gas.

"Yes," he said. "I remember that. Something about putting litmus paper in and it comes out blue."

Kokintz shook his head, but in resignation. "Yes," he said. "You put in litmus paper and it comes out blue. I know, as you know, that certain elements have an attraction for other elements. I know, for instance, that almost all metals have a kind of hunger for oxygen, which is why iron rusts and brass and copper tarnish, brass less than copper because it contains tin, which is less hungry for oxygen than copper. But it is the why that is always important. Why are so many elements hungry for oxygen? Why is there an affinity, as we call it, between some atoms and repulsion between others? Oh yes, we know now about atomic fields and nuclei. We know about the attraction between protons and neutrons and the other atomic particles.

"But I ask myself, 'Is it possible that in the nucleus of the oxygen atom there are certain particles, individually or in combinations, which are missing but which are common to the metallic atoms? Is it possible that the forces which result from such a theoretical absence of particles demand that atomic oxygen unite with a great variety of other elements to produce oxides of various kinds?' Of course, whatever goes on is likely to be much more complicated than this. I have selected a relatively simple starting point on which a great deal of work has already been done and is available to me…"

The rest of the exposition was mere sound to Mountjoy, who wondered now, as he had often wondered before, whether Kokintz was entirely sane. He did not subscribe to the theory of the vulgar that all scientists are mad, or that all scientists are absent-minded—though Kokintz very often was quite unconscious of what was going on around him. Many scientists he knew were not mad at all, particularly the English ones like Priestley and Rutherford. The French scientists like Pasteur and Lavoisier were, of course, a bit cracked as a result of being French.

But Dr. Kokintz at times showed signs, to Mountjoy's mind, of mental instability. Birds, penny whistles, mathematics, and whatever sort of messing around he was doing with the insides of atoms, made a curious melange. Each was, in itself, probably a perfectly sane and reasonable field of endeavor. But to mix them all up together in the way Kokintz did was eccentric, to say the least. Mountjoy, having endured an incomprehensible flow of words on the perfectly ordinary and acceptable fact that metals of all kinds rust, was a trifle impatient.

"Well," he said with a touch of sarcasm, "I don't want to detain you, but I think that you ought to seriously consider one of those memory banks of which I spoke. And perhaps several electron microscopes of various sizes of whatever they come in, and a completely new laboratory. Perhaps a computer would be of service. I believe they can now be built to individual specifications. You don't have to accept a stock model."

Kokintz shook his head. "No," he said. "Any time I have a problem I can refer it to Cal Tech or MIT and they solve it for me. A computer in Grand Fenwick? That's ridiculous."

Mountjoy had noted that one of the large stones of the walls had been removed, apparently by Kokintz, and was lying on top of a cardboard folder. "What's that for?" he asked, pointing to the stone.

"Oh, I am using it to make some pressings of leaves and flowers."

"We could buy you some kind of a press for that purpose, you know," said Mountjoy.

"Not necessary," said Kokintz. "The wall is six feet thick. To withstand cannon balls. There are no cannon balls these days and one stone taken out does no damage to it at all."

"Look here," said the Count. "There must be something of which you stand in immediate need and which we could order for you right away."

Kokintz reflected solemnly.

"There is," he said. "I would be very grateful for about ten bags of marbles ..."

Mountjoy, without waiting for the rest of the sentence, swept out of the study.

CHAPTER III

"Money," said the Count of Mountjoy, "far from being the root of all evil, as the vulgar suppose, represents a tremendous and touching expression of national and international faith and completely refutes the arguments of those cynics who maintain that world peace and prosperity are impossible because man is by nature distrustful, hostile, and conniving."

"We must abolish all taxes and leave the workingman with a full pay envelope for the first time in the history of this country," said Mr. David Bentner, leader of the Labor party of Grand Fenwick and therefore of the party in political opposition to Mountjoy.

Mountjoy ignored him. At this critical meeting of the Privy Council of the Duchy he was not going to argue politics with the tenacious and short-sighted Bentner.

"It follows," said Mountjoy, "that whoever destroys the value of money destroys the most precious possession of humanity—faith. He destroys the basis of all trade, the basis of all security, the basis of all government and the basis of all civilization."

"A full pay envelope and an end to taxation to support the wealthy," said Bentner doggedly. "That's my stand and I'm sticking to it."

"The destruction of money, in short," said Mountjoy, "means the destruction of faith. And the destruction of faith means an end to government and to civilization and the reemergence of barbarism."

"The money belongs to the workingman," said Bentner, not to be diverted by Mountjoy's soaring phrases, "and it must be given to him direct by a remission of taxes and a bonus at Christmastime—I'd say a five-hundred-shilling bonus for every family in the Duchy. Election coming up in spring," he added thoughtfully.

"Mr. Bentner," said the Count of Mountjoy severely, "I'm going to ask you a question which I think will make clear to you truths which are hidden from you at the present time." He took a slim gold wallet from the inside pocket of his morning coat and extracted from it a Grand Fenwick ten-shilling note.

"Now," he said, holding out the note for Bentner and the other members of the Privy Council to see, "what is that?"

"Ten-shilling note," said Bentner.

"Worth?" asked the Count.

"Ten shillings," said Bentner.

"And why is it worth ten shillings?" asked Mountjoy.

"That's easy. Printed right there on the face," said Bentner.

"Excellent," said Mountjoy. "Whatever is printed on the face of the note—that is the value of the note?"

"Right," said Bentner.

"Who says?" asked Mountjoy.

"Government, of course," said Bentner. "Her Grace"—bobbing his head in her direction—"they're her notes. Leastways they've got her picture on them. She says they're worth ten shillings or whatever is printed on the face of them and that's good enough for me."

"In short," said Mountjoy, "you, all of you here and all in Grand Fenwick, accept a piece of engraved paper as being worth ten shillings because you believe it is worth ten shillings. It is an act of faith on our part. Faith makes it worth ten shillings—faith alone."

"Pays a farm laborer's rent for one week and no more," snapped Bentner dourly. "Milk's ten pence a pint and going up too," he added.

"Supposing," said Mountjoy, "I were now to dump six million ten-shilling notes into the Duchy—divide them up among all the families in Grand Fenwick. That would give"—he scribbled for a while on a sheet of paper—"about six thousand ten-shilling notes to each head of a household in Grand Fenwick. Do you think then that a farm laborer would be able to rent a cottage for ten shillings a week?"

"Don't see why not," said Bentner, a little uncertain.

"You underestimate yourself," said Mountjoy sarcastically. "I am sure you can appreciate that if ten-shilling notes have become as plentiful as pennies, no landlord will put a cottage to rent for a week for so miserable a sum as ten shillings. He will want twenty or thirty or forty shillings."

"What's wrong with that?" asked Bentner. "If everybody has lots of money, it won't make any difference."

"What happens to the wages of a man who is earning, say, forty shillings a week?" countered the Count.

"He'll have to have more," said Bentner. "And I and my party will see that he gets more," he added aggressively.

"Ah," said Mountjoy. "But suppose the value of what he produces to sell abroad—wine or wool—is less than the wages he is being paid to produce it—what then?"

Bentner opened his mouth a couple of times to reply and then lapsed into frustrated silence, conscious that the Count had once more encouraged him to run full tilt down a blind alley.

"The known saying should be amended to 'The abuse of money is the root of all evil,' " said the Count of Mountjoy, addressing the Council at large. "And money is abused when it is made so common as to lose its value, or when its relation to production becomes so erratic that the public loses confidence in it, which is really the same thing. Faith is the essence of monetary value, and when faith is destroyed, economic anarchy is at hand."

"Look here," said Bentner, who had recovered from his setback. "Nobody is advocating taking six thousand ten-shilling notes and giving them to the head of every household in the Duchy. All I'm asking is that taxes be abolished for a couple of years so that the workingman can have the full benefit of his labor in his pay envelope."

"Mr. Bentner," said Mountjoy, "far be it from me to counsel you on next year's election since we are of opposite political persuasions. But if nobody in the Duchy is paying any taxes at election time next spring, how do you expect to interest the voters in your party's program?"

Bentner relapsed into silence again.

Mountjoy addressed himself to Gloriana. "I had not wished to bring this problem before Your Grace's Council without having a solution to propose," he said. "I do not deem it the function of my office to produce problems without solving them. I regret that I have but a partial solution to put before you to the present problem of this unwarranted surfeit of money, though I have reviewed all the historic methods of dealing with unwanted money surpluses employed by other nations."

"You mean we are not the first nation in history to have too much money dumped on us?" asked Gloriana.

"Not by any means, Your Grace," said Mountjoy. "The problem has been common to the United States of America, for instance, since the end of the Second World War. It is a problem which democracies in particular have difficulty in solving, though the older monarchies were well able to cope with it. The extravagances of the court and the aristocracy in Tzarist Russia and Royalist France, for instance, could be relied upon to get rid of all the surplus money in the kingdom and much which was by no means surplus—without ruining the national fiscal system. Alas, with democracies the task is not so easy, for there is no select group into whose hands the surplus funds can be channeled without damage to the nation's banking and trade."

"What do the Americans do with their surplus money?" asked Gloriana, intrigued.

"First they collect it into the government coffers by taxation," said Mountjoy. "They are the most adroit nation in the world in devising taxes. A nation which came into being in a rebellion against taxes has become the Machiavelli of the politics of taxation. The money, taken out of the hands of potential spenders in the amount of billions of dollars a month, cannot then be spent by the government itself in the United States. That government is then at the point at which we ourselves now stand—confronted with a surplus of money and the problem of getting rid of it without returning it to the economy.

"Their situation, however, is less difficult than ours. A nation of such size and power and prestige in the world can give away large quantities of money in various foreign-aid programs which may improve matters abroad, may make others friendly toward the United States—though that result has not yet become manifest—but will certainly get rid of the greater part of the embarrassing money surplus without it getting back into the national economy."

"Just a minute," said Tully Bascomb. "If these gifts of money abroad are in dollar credits, then the dollars will surely eventually find their way back into the United States."

"True," said Mountjoy. "But there is huge wastage in the process. And there is a very beneficent time lapse between the time when the money is sent abroad and the time it gets back. It comes back slowly, and during the interval various measures can be undertaken to improve the economic picture at home."

"Meaning more taxes," said Bentner.

"Usually meaning more taxes," said Mountjoy.

"Couldn't we have some kind of foreign-aid program?" asked Gloriana. "What about the Irish? Nobody's done anything for them for centuries. Why not just give them a million dollars with our very best wishes—at Christmas?"

"Better not to meddle," said Mountjoy. "Such a gift might hint at an alliance between the Republic of Ireland and the Duchy of Grand Fenwick which would seriously disturb the six counties of Northern Ireland which still remain loyal to William of Orange."

"William of Orange?" cried Gloriana. "He's been dead since the early eighteenth century."

"Quite so," said Mountjoy. "But he still rules in British Ireland. No, it's best not to think of a foreign-aid program. Whatever benefits might result would be offset by international entanglements which we, as a completely neutral nation, cannot afford."

"What else do the Americans do?" asked Gloriana.

"They use the slow-down method," said Mountjoy. "They collect, say, two hundred billion dollars in the tax year, spend a hundred billion abroad either on goodwill or warfare, and rely on there being quite a while before that money trickles back again into their own economy. Then they use government bonds with a fixed interest rate which cannot be cashed for a stated period—this mops up surplus currency. Also they undertake vast government projects at home. For instance, the United States has the biggest civil service known to man—more people at higher wages for perhaps less work than has ever before been achieved. This, though roundly cursed by the taxpayer, constitutes a tremendous protection for him for it represents a huge money-absorbing machine, which sucks up billions and allows them to drip back into the economy only slowly. Cries for economy in government are really pleas for a vast national disaster, though few realize this. Any American President or Congress who cut the budget in half would send the nation into an inflationary spiral from which it might never recover.

"The Americans have, moreover, one further weapon which is denied us and is the master tool of capitalism. And that is an increasing number of products. With more and more things to buy on the market every day, there are more and more outlets for the spending of money, and the relationship between dollars and produce is kept relatively stable. In our case, however, our national product is fixed in both variety and quantity. But our national revenue has soared as a result of these terrible earnings from chewing gum. Thus here in Grand Fenwick, if this money is allowed to get into the hands of our people, the price of everything will soar, which is another way of saying that the value of our pound will fall disastrously. In essence there must be a steady and fixed relationship between produce and money or money becomes of less and less use until trade has to be conducted by barter."

"You mentioned that you have a partial solution," said

Gloriana. "What is it?"

"I think we can reduce taxes from twelve to eight percent and make up the deficit out of these American funds. Then we can insist that Dr. Kokintz spend two hundred thousand dollars on equipment for himself whether he needs it or not. If we ordered very expensive scientific paraphernalia from America (it will serve them right to get their dollars sent back) and then have it sent here by common freighter and uninsured, there is a very good chance that it will be so hopelessly damaged by the time it arrives that Dr. Kokintz will not have to bother with it, since he doesn't want it in the first place. We could also air-condition the whole castle. But I have to confess that after going into the whole problem as fully as I am able, I find we will still have about six hundred thousand dollars left over with no method in sight by which it may be got rid of."

He paused and then continued gravely. "I have to warn Your Grace that this is only the beginning of future troubles which may, alas, destroy that complete independence and neutrality which we have fostered in this country for six hundred years. Our profits from the chewing gum were one million dollars this year. Next year they may be two millions. The year after five. And what are we to do in those circumstances I cannot envisage."

"We will have to give that chewing-gum factory and all our rights in the manufacture of the chewing gum away," said Tully. "That is obvious and we must start to work on that immediately."

"We could just close it down, couldn't we?" asked Gloriana. "Haven't we the right to do that?"

Mountjoy shook his head. "We can neither give it away nor close it down for ten years," he said. "Under the original agreement, to protect the investment of the American lessees, we gave them a guarantee that they would have the right to manufacture and sell the gum for twenty-five years, and our contract with them runs for that period."

"What fathead cooked that one up?" asked Bentner, who very much disliked these lectures by Mountjoy.

"It was cooked up, as you put it, between the United States Secretary of State, Her Grace, Duchess Gloriana XII, and myself as her chief adviser," said Mountjoy. "It was approved by the Senate of the United States and our own Council of Freemen." He turned to Bentner and added smoothly, "Quite a number of fatheads, as you see, had a hand in the affair." Bentner ignored that. "Do you mean to tell me that we are bound by international treaty to make and sell this gum in the United States?"

"That is so," said Mountjoy. "The terms were incorporated in the Treaty of Peace between ourselves and the Americans. Such a provision is not so uncommon," he said, turning to the Duchess. "The peace treaty for Austria at the close of World War Two deals with the staffing of the police department and the fire brigade in Trieste."

"Maybe we are overlooking a very obvious solution," said Tully. "Why not just leave the money in the United States in a bank or invested in bonds? Surely there's nothing that demands that we bring it to Grand Fenwick and flood the country with it?"

"We can't do that because we could never keep it secret," said Mountjoy. "The funds would mount enormously for we can expect tremendous profits each year. The time would inevitably arrive when news of our dollar holdings would be made public and our people would come to realize that the government was the possessor of the wealth of Midas. The demand that the people themselves be allowed to share in that wealth either in whole or in a generous part would prove irresistible. And we would then be ruined."

"Look here," said Bentner, "I don't agree with that. I say let us take this money and apply the whole of it to tax relief. Let us abolish income tax and every kind of tax in Grand Fenwick. Why not, if the money's available? Why should people have to pay taxes?"

He had been scribbling on a scratch pad on the table before him and he said, "With the money we have coming now we could abolish income tax in Grand Fenwick for three years. And with what comes in next year, we could abolish it for three years more. In fact, we could probably abolish income tax in our country for all time. And that's what I say should be done. Use the money for running the country and let the workingman have a full pay envelope for the first time in his life."

"I'm inclined to agree with Mr. Bentner," said Gloriana.

"And I too," said Tully. "Let's use the money to abolish taxes."

"This will be a grave mistake," said Mountjoy. "I am firmly of the opinion that unless people make a money contribution to their government, they will lose interest in their government. They will not care how money is spent or how policies are followed since their own purses are not involved."

"Let us try it as a half-measure at present," said Gloriana. "Let us announce to the people the receipt of this money. I think it wrong to withhold the information from them—and let us propose in the Council of Freemen when Mountjoy presents his new budget that all taxes be immediately reduced by fifty percent, with the prospect that they will be entirely eliminated in the future if the financial situation warrants."

A vote was taken and proved to be three to one in favor of this solution.

CHAPTER IV

The Council of Freemen of Grand Fenwick was one of the most ancient parliamentary bodies in Europe. It readily predated the famed House of Keys on the Isle of Man and was modeled wisely on the British Parliament with its upper house composed of the Lords both Spiritual and Temporal, and the lower house, or Council of Freemen, the elected representatives of the voters. The upper house could veto laws but could not propose them, and its power of veto could be exercised only twice on any given piece of legislature. On such a law passing the Council of Freemen a third time, it had automatically to be passed by the House of Nobles and signed by the Duchess, who was a constitutional monarch with carefully limited powers.

News of the Duchy's windfall of dollars had, following the meeting of the Privy Council, been allowed to get abroad, and the whole nation, in the midst of multiplying rumors, awaited the Count's budget message, which would reveal what was to be done with this splendid bonus. The amount of the money was first underestimated, then correctly gauged, and then grossly overestimated until there were some who believed that they would be the masters of a fortune of ten thousand dollars apiece (the equivalent for most of ten years' wages) as soon as Mountjoy brought forth his budget proposals.

Bentner, it is regrettable to report, rather fostered this kind of speculation. He was anxious that the whole of the sum be spent on the workingman, part in tax relief and part in the form of a back bonus. Bentner believed that if he got the expectations of the workingman up high enough, Mountjoy would not dare withhold any part of the sum (as was now proposed) but would have to give the whole amount to the voters in one form or another.

Believing then that a substantial money gift was to come to them from the United States, many in Grand Fenwick became quite sentimental about Americans. American flags appeared here and there in windows, and at the sign of The Crooked Stick (a reference to Grand Fenwick's national weapon, the longbow) there were some who ventured to say that the United States Marines, given a little training, might without a blush stand shoulder to shoulder on the field of battle with the men-at-arms of Grand Fenwick.

Plans for spending the money were eagerly discussed. Some would refurnish their houses; others, rebuild portions of them or add a room or two. Mail orders for new bicycles (the only form of transportation other than horses available or permitted in Grand Fenwick) were huge, and even before a dollar of the delightful money had arrived in the Duchy, Sid Cromer, who ran a blacksmith forge and bicycle-repair shop in the town which surrounded the castle, complained that he was being ruined.

"Not a damaged sprocket or a broken chain in a week," he said to Bentner, waving under the latter's nose a stubby forefinger grimy with dirty machine oil. "Who wants to repair anything when they can get it new? Answer me that."

"Take it easy, Sid," said Bentner. "You'll be getting yours too, you know. And with all those new bicycles coming in, business should double for you in a couple of months."

"I don't know about that," said Mr. Cromer. "I've had five shillings every two months regular from the Derby family for fixing brakes and handlebars. Ten kids in that family and two bicycles both with bent frames. Makes for something regular that I can count on and that's what I like."

"Well, there'll be ten kids and ten bicycles in a little while," said Bentner. "Don't worry. They'll be in to have things fixed. If you gave those Derby kids a hammer apiece they'd destroy half of Europe in six months."

Cromer went back into his shop, where he sat for a while, surrounded by fading advertisements for Lucas headlights, BSA sport kits, and Willhold handgrips, while he thought over the future of the bicycle business in Grand Fenwick. Then he washed his hands in a pan of dirty kerosene, wiped them on his overalls, and went over to see Bob Davis at the Fenwick Home Bank, which shared its premises with a candy store run by a lady known to everybody as Aunt Tettie.

"What can I do for you, Sid?" asked the bank manager.

"Well," said Sid, "I want to draw out all my money."

"Why?" asked Davis, blanching slightly, for Mr. Cromer was one of the heaviest depositors.

"Don't know much about money," said the other, "but if everybody in Grand Fenwick is going to get themselves a new bicycle, I'd do better to put my money into bicycle parts than leave it in the bank."

"True," said Mr. Davis. "But I can lend you all you need for bicycle parts. You don't have to touch your capital."

"Why should I borrow money when I already have money?" asked the mechanic. "Answer me that."

Mr. Davis took a little while to consider the correct phrasing with which to answer this question, which had been put to him many times before. It was remarkable how few people understood that you could not borrow money unless you had money—that credit was dependent on capital and you could not summon capital into being by borrowing—even some of the greatest corporations in the United States of America did not understand that.

"If you use your capital to buy bicycle parts," he said, "you have frozen your money in a particular kind of asset which you may be able to sell at a profit, or you may have to sell at a loss, which means selling your money at a discount. Supposing, for instance, people started ordering parts for their bicycles through the mail instead of from you. They might have to wait a little longer, but they might get them cheaper that way. Then you would be stuck with all your money tied up in bicycle parts which you could not sell. Or you might order a quantity of one kind of part only to find that another kind, which you did not have in stock, was needed. In any case, you are risking your money by turning it into a speculative asset which you may not be able to turn into money again very readily.

"Now if you use borrowed money and the same thing happens—there is no market for your bicycle parts immediately—you owe the bank a certain sum plus interest. However, you have a lot of time in which to pay back the loan. That time gives you an opportunity of disposing of the bicycle parts. To be sure, the interest you must pay the bank for the loan will cut into your profits unless you can mark up the price of the parts so as to include your bank interest; that is, pass the interest on to the customer. Remember that time is money. Things that are worth money are often valueless or sold at far below their value because there is not time to turn them into money. Borrowing provides times as well as cash since the loan can be repaid over a long trading period.

"Finally, if you borrow the money for your parts, instead of using your own capital, you still have your capital behind you. And I could, of course, lend you far more money than you have on deposit in the bank, so borrowing provides more money than your own capital provides."

Cromer considered this, rubbing the side of his nose with a forefinger from which the kerosene had by no means removed all the dirt.

"You can lend me more than I have on deposit?" he asked with a measure of slyness.

"Yes," said Davis.

"And the same goes, I suppose, for everybody else. You're not making an exception in my case, I'm sure."

"Quite true."

"Well, how can you lend to your depositors more money than they have on deposit in the bank?" asked the mechanic. "That would use up all the money in the bank and more. Isn't that true?"

"Not at all," said Mr. Davis. "Actual physical money is not involved. If you wanted to borrow a thousand pounds, you would not want to receive that money in your hands, would you? You wouldn't have a safe place to keep it to start with. No. I would credit a thousand pounds to your account and…"

"You mean you wouldn't actually take money out of your vaults and put it in the place where you keep mine?" asked the mechanic.

"Not at all," said Davis, smiling at so simple a concept. "All I do is write in your account a credit of one thousand Grand Fenwick pounds. You can spend that amount from your account at any time, though you probably would not spend it all at once. The same with other borrowers. They would also get a credit on their accounts of the amount of their loan—a figure written there indicating the amount of the bank's money they can borrow at that time.

"Meanwhile, all the money deposited in the bank is still there except for the daily deposits and withdrawals of cash, and the bank is able to operate profitably on the interest received from the loans and also the investments which it itself may make with the money deposited by its clients."

"Just a minute," said Sid. "Supposing I write a check to the Lucas Company of England for twenty pounds for bicycle lamps. I get the lamps. They get the check. The check comes back to you. You deduct twenty pounds from my balance. And then you have to send twenty pounds to the Lucas Company in England—or to their bank. Right?"

"Wrong," said the manager. "All that happens is that your balance is debited by the figure of twenty pounds and the account of the Lucas Company with their bank in England is credited with twenty pounds. No actual exchange of cash takes place immediately at all."

"So it's just figures that banks write in books?" asked Cromer.

Mr. Davis nodded.

There was a silence while Sid Cromer absorbed the economic procedure with which he had been confronted. "All right," he said. "How much money can you lend me?"

"Whatever you wish," said Davis. "It will be at six percent."

"Fair enough," said Sid. "Lend me two thousand pounds, and I am going to need five hundred of that in cash."

The papers were soon drawn and signed and five one-hundred-pound notes counted into his hand. Sid thanked the bank manager, left, and dropped in at The Crooked Stick, where he had a meditative glass of wine before the fire in the saloon bar.

Then he went back to his shop and tore down all the faded and oil-grimed signs dealing with bicycles and bicycle parts. He found a piece of board and a pot of paint and worked with these materials for a while. And when he was done, he hung over his shop a sign which read:

FENWICK NATIONAL BANK AND BIKE SHOP
Get Your Loans Here

CHAPTER V

The Count of Mountjoy suffered his first budget defeat in twenty years over what was now known in the Duchy as the Gum Money. His budget proposals were in every aspect reasonable. But inflamed by Bentner, who rightly saw an opportunity of overthrowing the government, the Council of Freemen voted them down.

The proposals were that the rate of income tax be reduced to 5 percent, that the deficit be made up with Gum Money, that a hundred thousand dollars' worth of the same money be spent on equipping a completely new laboratory for Dr. Kokintz whether he wished it or not, that a further four hundred thousand dollars be spent on air-conditioning the castle of Grand Fenwick, Americans only being employed on that project, that each taxpayer be given a Christmas gift of seventy-five dollars (twenty-five pounds), and that the remainder of the money be sent as a gift to Columbia University in New York to set up a department of Grand Fenwick Studies in that eminent institution.

The Count of Mountjoy, before appearing before the Council of Freemen, was well aware that his budget was not brilliant and had but little hope of acceptance. It was an effort of desperation, the best that he could devise, and he consoled himself that the problem he faced would have baffled Keynes, Montagu, Smith, or any of the other great economic theorists of the world.

What, he wondered, would happen in Britain or America if the equivalent of the total national budget for five or six years was dumped suddenly into the nation's treasury? With an unexpected budget surplus of perhaps 600 percent, how could any nation resist the demand for the utter abolition of taxation and a sharing of the wealth among all the citizens?

No. Mountjoy knew that he was to go down to defeat, but he knew also that the budget he had drawn up or something like it was needed. For the national interest demanded that the money be got rid of and not allowed to flow into the nation's economy.

Bentner had himself perceived this dimly and for a short while. But no man whose political life has been spent in an unceasing struggle for higher wages for the workers can turn away from so tremendous a windfall. As Mountjoy remarked, the views on money of those who merely earn it will never coincide with the views on money of those who spend their time making it out of their production and business. The one will always demand more. The other may well sometimes demand less in the interest of preserving its value.

The little sop which Mountjoy felt he could offer the voters—a Christmas gift of twenty-five pounds each—could not avert his overthrow. He presented his budget to a tense, irritated and supercritical House, and the hoots and jeers which greeted his offer were felt by some to be quite unworthy of the traditions of that chamber. In the days which preceded the budget presentation, however, the people had come to expect a vast fortune, and the Count's offer struck even representatives of the Council as close to an insult.

The vote against acceptance of the budget was overwhelming—thirty-three to seven, for even many members of Mountjoy's own party crossed the floor to vote against him. Mountjoy, almost deserted, after the vote was taken and announced, looked in silence about the crowded Council chamber, with its ancient walls of golden Fenwick oak paneling and its yew benches, some of which dated from the late sixteenth century. Draped from the walls, above the heads of the delegates, were the battle banners of the Duchy's knights—foremost among them, of course, the double-headed eagle of the Duchy, saying "Aye" from one beak and "Nay" from the other.

Side by side with this was the Sunburst banner of Mountjoy and the Pickerels gules on a field azure of the Cromers and the Red Hand, coupe, of the Dermots of Ballycastle (the only Irish strain in Grand Fenwick) and so on. They represented a great deal of tradition and of courage, those banners, of honor and of loyalty. There was in them what required to be preserved not merely for Grand Fenwick but for the world at large. And it was with a heavy heart that the Count realized that the defeat he had been handed by the delegates to the Council of Freemen was a vote for self rather than for nation and not in accordance with the tradition of the country.

Though defeated, Mountjoy would not retract his stand. "The government acknowledges its overwhelming defeat on the issue of the national budget," he said when the vote was taken. "And honorable members may be assured that I will, at the first appropriate moment, submit my resignation to Her Grace, so that arrangements may be immediately put in hand for a general election.

"I would, however, be lacking in my duty if I did not solemnly warn this Council now, and the people of the Duchy, that there are values which must be put ahead of money and of self if any nation or any civilization is to survive. Public welfare must always come ahead of private need, and this maxim, honored in the past, has, I fear, been thrown aside in the present vote. In the coming election I shall continue, however, to strongly oppose the introduction of these dollar earnings into our economy on the sound grounds that they will destroy first the value of our own currency and then the value of our own labor. For what man, I ask you, will work hard all year for a thousand shillings when he may receive the same sum by remaining idle for twelve months?

"I would charge all of you to bear in mind that all societies exist through the efforts and work of their members and no society can exist where the members expect to receive without giving. I would recall to the memory of honorable members the words of the famous president of a young country, slain in office, on the occasion of his inauguration, 'Ask not what your country can do for you; ask what you can do for your country.' There is guidance there for all men at all times and especially for us now in Grand Fenwick."

He paused and then, looking with scorn at those members of his own party who had crossed the floor to vote against him, said, "I am reminded, gentlemen, by your presence on the opposition benches of Browning's rebuke to Wordsworth. I take the liberty of paraphrasing the words:

"Just for a handful of silver, you left me,
Just for a dollar to put in your coat..."

In silence he shut the scarlet leather dispatch box before him and handed it to the Speaker of the House. The gesture symbolized his resignation as Head of the Government, and then he walked from the Council, followed by the six of his party who had remained loyal to him.

An election was now inevitable—an election to be held at the very worst time of the year for Grand Fenwick, that is, during the grape harvest. Before the election the Count of Mountjoy called formally on the Duchess to submit his resignation, which she was obliged to accept, although she was very fond of the Count.

"Bobo, is it really this serious?" she asked him. "Will Grand Fenwick really be endangered by this money being put into circulation?"

"Yes, Your Grace," said the Count. "There will be an immediate effect on our economy which, however, will be trivial compared with the lasting effects which can be expected from millions of dollars a year being dumped into our country, without anybody in Grand Fenwick doing a tap of work toward earning this fortune."

"Millions a year?" queried the Duchess.

"Yes, Your Grace," said the Count. "Millions a year. For this is just the start. Each year we can expect more profits from the gum. And our people, having once taken that money to spend as they wish, are not likely at another time to turn it away and say they do not want it. We are seeing the last days of Grand Fenwick as it used to be—a sturdy, self-sufficient, independent nation with a heritage of which any country in the world could be proud. We are likely to become, now that Bentner is having his way, a nation of ne'er-do-wells, of slackers and idlers.

"There is the workingman's dream come to its logical fruition—no work, plenty of pay and rule by ignorance." He paused and added solemnly, "We may even produce some kind of group like the Beatles, noted for complaining to the accompaniment of guitars." This thought was so painful that the Count of Mountjoy, having uttered the words, closed his eyes as a man in an agony of shame.

"You're kidding," said the Duchess, herself so deeply shaken that she was guilty of an Americanism.

Bentner, summoned later to the Ducal presence, took a more cheerful view. Since he was leader of the Labor party, which was opposed to titles, he could not bring himself to call Gloriana Your Grace, as did the Count of Mountjoy. But he called her "Ma'am," which delighted Gloriana as being cozier. She was quite as fond of Bentner, rotund, stubborn, plodding, as she was of the graceful and agile Count of Mountjoy.

"Don't you fret about it, Ma'am," said Bentner, when she mentioned the Count's fears to him. "The upper classes are always afraid of what the lower classes will do if they get their hands on some money. You'd think money was dynamite, the way they want to keep it away from people."

"If you should win the election, Mr. Bentner, what will you propose doing with the money?" asked Gloriana.

"Give some to Kokintz for what he needs. And divide the rest of it among the voters."

"Which will give most of them the equivalent of a year's wages for nothing," said the Duchess. "Do you think that is wise? Will they work if they get money so freely?"

"Of course they'll work," said Bentner. "They're used to working. It is the rich who are used to idleness. They'll work, Ma'am. You can be sure of that. But they'll live in better houses and have better clothing. That's what most of the money will go on. They'll have now the things that otherwise they would have to save twenty years to get."

"And what happens next year—and the year after?" asked the Duchess.

"That'll have to take care of itself, Ma'am," said Bentner. "We haven't any guarantee that there will be any money from America next year. The Americans might start smoking again." A brilliant idea occurred to him suddenly. "One of the first things we should do when we have a new government is to write to the Surgeon General of the United States and congratulate him on his courageous war against the perils of nicotine."

"Mr. Bentner," said Gloriana primly, "I believe you smoke yourself."

"A pipe, Ma'am," said Bentner piously. "No harm in a pipe."

Mountjoy waged as staunch a campaign as he could for the return of his party to power, but he had no chance of winning the election. He found that everybody was prepared to listen to his warnings against the evils of inflation. But nobody seemed to think that these warnings applied to themselves. Places like Britain, France, Germany, Italy and the United States, they agreed, might contract the sophisticated financial disease called inflation, but not Grand Fenwick, where people were far too sensible and too self-controlled for such afflictions.

Bentner, promising hundreds in cash and no taxation, was swept into office in a landslide vote that left Mountjoy with but three supporters in the new Council of Freemen. Indeed, he scarcely saved his party from extinction and to do so even dragged Dr. Kokintz into politics by making the great scientist speak out against dividing the Gum Money among the voters.

After the election, which made Bentner Prime Minister of the Duchy, Mountjoy grimly awaited the passing of the new budget and its effect on the economy of the Duchy.

The effects were not entirely what he had expected.

Most of the money divided among the voters immediately left the Duchy. It was spent on things the Duchy did not produce—bicycles, as noted, also washing machines and dishwashers and television sets (though reception in the Duchy was abominable due both to the mountains and to the electrical conditions which enveloped them). The money slipped through people's hands very fast. It made life in Grand Fenwick infinitely more exciting and glamorous for a while. There were great discussions among the housewives on the virtues of particular washing machines and tremendous pressure on the government to start generating electricity immediately (for the Duchy was without electric power and so, of course, the washing machines could not be worked—the television sets were battery-operated).

Unfortunately, Bentner had not thought that one result of the dollar windfall would be a demand for electricity in Grand Fenwick. There were no funds in the Treasury for establishing a generating plant. However, the demand was such (for the housewives of the Duchy, not unnaturally, wanted to see their washing machines, in whose possession they took such pride, actually working) that a bill was rushed through the Council of Freemen, permitting the Duchy to borrow from the Home Bank sufficient funds to start a power station. The money, of course, would have to be repaid out of taxes; so hidden in the electricity bill was a clause calling for an increase in the income tax of 3 percent.

It was only after the passing of several weeks that the secondary and more lasting effects of the windfall became apparent in Grand Fenwick. They were all surprising. One was an increase in income tax to pay for the cost of a power station. Another was an increase in the private debts of individual citizens. Householders found themselves pressed by their families to make many purchases and decided to borrow money, since the bonus they had received would not cover all that was needed. They went to Mr. Davis at the Home Bank and he explained that if they would open an account with him and make a substantial deposit he might be able to lend them quite a bit more than they had in their accounts.

(Sid Cromer, who had added banking to his bicycle-repairing business, was also able to make some loans, but since he was borrowing money from Davis, he had to charge a higher rate of interest and so got as clients only those of dubious credit who had been turned down by the banker.)

Side by side with this increase in private debt there was an increase in prices throughout the Duchy. Landlords, finding they now had to make monthly payments for their purchases financed by the bank, raised their rents. Farmers, finding their rented land higher in price, raised the price of milk and vegetables. Laborers and working people, finding they had to pay more for food and for rent of their homes, demanded an increase of earnings.

Six months, then, after the overthrow of the Mountjoy government and the sharing of the Gum Money among the people there were ugly rumors of strikes among the agricultural workers of

Grand Fenwick. A small hydroelectric generating plant had been installed and the people found that, having had to pay for its erection in the first place, they now had to pay for its product in the second. To their regular bills was now added an electricity bill. And to provide the hot water for their washing machines and dishwashers they had to go further into debt in installing water heaters. Many had no plumbing other than a kitchen pump, so there were more bills for plumbing. Indeed, in the Duchy only two men prospered—Mr. Davis, the bank manager, and Sid Cromer, the bicycle-repair man.

Sid, however, had found that banking was beyond him. His loans went sour and he was burdened with debts. But his bicycle business picked up enormously. And he found a completely new field of endeavor in repairing dishwashers and washing machines. He made far more money than he had made before, despite his debts. But he worked far harder than he had worked before.

By the following summer, then, the people of Grand Fenwick had achieved an enormously higher standard of living, with hot and cold running water in every house, with electric light, television, washing machines, and new bicycles. (They liked the commercials, telling them of products they had never seen, rather more than the programs, which were dull by comparison. Puffing their cigarettes, they cheered those which warned of the dangers of smoking.)

However, for the first time in the Duchy's history, everybody had money troubles. Only Dr. Kokintz, who had managed to get three gross of colored marbles out of the Gum Money, was unperturbed. He worked away happily constructing his curious models with his marbles, smoking his big Oompaul pipe, chatting with his birds and obligingly repairing television sets whenever required. If he thought anything about the money crisis, he said nothing.

Mountjoy, like Achilles, remained in his tent. But with this difference—as the Duchy's troubles mounted, he was smiling.

CHAPTER VI

Demands for payment of estimated income tax in Grand Fenwick went out each midsummer, dropping their little dollop of gloom into the holiday period (as they do in other nations). The Grand Fenwick tax, before the arrival and disbursal of the Gum Money, had been paid in advance only by those who were self-employed. It was now levied on all who had received a share of the money and these were outraged to discover that they were required to pay taxes on the unexpected bonus they had received.

None had put aside any portion of the money to pay taxes. A cry of wrath swept from one end of the Duchy to the other. The people remembered that Bentner had promised during the election to abolish income tax. To a man they announced that they were hanged if they were going to pay a penny in tax on money which had been received as an outright gift. It was in vain for Bentner to argue that the decision whether a sum of money was a gift or an earning depended not on its nature but on the government's need for funds.

If the government needed money, then life itself was not a gift but an earning and must be taxed. The people of Grand Fenwick would not hear of such arguments. They refused to pay any tax on the bonus they had received and through their representatives in the Council of Freemen they demanded that these funds be always and forever tax-free.

Bentner tried to reason with them. He addressed a meeting of voters and taxpayers in the Common Hall of the castle and put the matter to them bluntly.

"Whether you like it or not," he said, "the government has to repay the loan made to finance the power plant. The money to do that cannot come out of thin air. It has to be provided by you, the taxpayer. So you'll just have to divvy up and console yourselves with the thought that there will be more money coming to you later on. My information is," he added cautiously, "that perhaps twice the amount of Gum Money will be available this year as last."

He should not have made this statement for the fact of the matter was that he had no such information at all. But the temptation to appear in a good light before the voters was too strong to overcome. The statement was made and it was met with such cheers that Bentner himself grew a little frightened and Mountjoy was completely aghast.

When the cheering had subsided there still remained the matter of paying the tax on the money already received. Mr. Jack Derby, father of that famous family of Derby children responsible for most of the breakage in the Duchy, returned to this question. He had not a penny left of the money he had got. He had instead debts, unpaid taxes, ten broken bicycles, four television sets of which only one worked and that spasmodically, and a great number of household appliances which his children in their enthusiasm had reduced largely to wreckage.

"If twice as much money is coming as has already been received," he said, "then let the government hold out the back taxes and the current taxes on that money before dividing it up among us. No sense giving us money and then making us hand some of it back, to my way of thinking."

There was a great deal of support at the meeting for this suggestion, and Bentner was forced to promise to take it under advisement. Actually he began to sense dimly that the government was in serious financial trouble. Receipts of revenue had actually fallen off, for many in their enthusiasm for spending had neglected to pay their regular bills. Government expenditure had, of course, increased, for the power station, once built, had to be kept in operation and that called for a staff of operating and servicing employees. And the government was now required for the first time to pay interest on its operating funds.

The money problems, Bentner admitted, made his head buzz. And what made his head buzz even more was the look of almost angelic pleasure on the face of the Count of Mountjoy whenever they met.

"The Century of the Common Man indeed," said the Count, quoting a favorite phrase of Bentner's. "Money on every hand, a chicken in every pot and not a soul in the Duchy who isn't burdened with debt, the government included. My dear Bentner, are you beginning now to see the wisdom of leaving the handling of money to the moneyed classes, who have generations of training in the field?"

"Can't expect people who have been deprived of money for centuries by the privileged few to use it wisely when they first get it," retorted Bentner. "Next year will see a difference, mark my words."

Meanwhile something had to be done about getting money into the Treasury immediately to cover the government's increased expenses. Also an arrangement had to be made with the bank to defer payment of the power station loan installment. Bentner went to the bank to explore the prospects of a further loan to the government against expected receipts both from taxes and from further gum earnings.

But the bank manager shook his head. "We're overextended," he said. "Between loans to the government and loans to private individuals, we have reached the end of our lending power. We can't extend a penny more in credit. However, it might be possible to borrow from other banks—in France or in England. That has been done before, you know. Though you will have to expect a pretty high rate of interest."

"How much?" asked Bentner.

"About eight percent."

"That doesn't bother me much," said Bentner. "In a few months' time we will have some more Gum Money coming in."

"Which you will have to divide up once more among the taxpayers," said Davis.

"After first paying off the government's debts," said Bentner.

"It seems to me, Mr. Bentner," said Davis, "that you are on the first upward curve of the well-known inflationary spiral. You are borrowing money for more than the money is worth. You are further depreciating the value of the money by spreading it out among the people of the Duchy, who are spending it with very little regard to their own earnings. I have been going over my books and if there were no Gum Money coming in next year, it would take the average wage earner in Grand Fenwick three years to get himself out of debt to my bank, provided that he didn't find in the interim that he had to borrow more money.

"As a banker I am, of course, interested in lending money at interest as a sound investment and a legitimate way of making money. But the craze for spending which these funds have set off in Grand Fenwick is not economically healthy. None of the spending increases the national product. The spending produces nothing, in fact, but the devaluation of our currency.

"It is my opinion—and I am so reporting to my directors in London—that Grand Fenwick is poised on the precipice of financial disaster and may plunge over at any moment."

"But when the new money comes in, everything will straighten out," said Bentner. "Surely you can see that if we collectively owe a million dollars and we have two million dollars coming to us, we are financially sound and have, in fact, a million-dollar capital free of debt."

"What I can plainly see," said Davis, "is that if another million dollars comes into the Duchy and is divided among the taxpayers, the present troubles will be four times as great by this time next year."

"With the taxes paid first of all—before the money is divided?" asked Bentner.

"Even with the taxes paid. For that money bears no relationship at all to work or to produce. It is gift money, which devalues earned money. You have already had a warning about this in the demands of the agricultural workers for higher pay. I might add that I have had to turn down requests for loans against next year's wool clip and grape harvest—loans I would have been pleased to make in the past."

"Why have you had to turn them down?" demanded Bentner.

"Because I have no guarantee whatever that laborers will clip the wool or gather the grapes at current wages, now devalued. And if their wages are raised, the margin of profit from wool and grapes will be smaller, and so the loan is too risky to make. I believe the needed money is being sought elsewhere."

"You mean in foreign banks?"

"Precisely," said Davis. "They will sometimes make loans which I cannot, having a wider operation which diminishes the risk of loss. Of course, if the creditors do not make good on the payments, then the banks involved would be able to take possession of the vineyards."

"You mean foreigners would own the vineyards of Grand

Fenwick?" asked Bentner, aghast.

"Precisely," said the bank manager. "Now as to the payment which is now due on the power station loan . ."

But Bentner was not listening. Nothing in the whole financial imbroglio had cut so sharply and painfully through the comforting maze of quasi-understanding in which he operated as the thought that foreign capital (two words which were equally repulsive to him) might own the precious vineyards of Grand Fenwick. He had heard of something of the sort happening in the Burgundy region of France—the taking over by foreign interests, in return for loans, of some of the great vineyards of the Cote d'Azur. There were rumors of the addition of synthetics to the mash to produce more wine more quickly, and horrifying stories of third-cutting grapes being added to the first cut to bulk them out. If Grand Fenwick lost her vineyards, then she lost both her livelihood and her pride.

Bentner walked in a daze from the bank manager's office and called in at The Crooked Stick for a glass of Pinot to pull together the shattered fibers of his confidence. A glass of Pinot used to cost sixpence, but Ed Teller, the innkeeper, now charged eight pence and the wine had a distinctly weak taste, lacking the authority of genuine Pinot.

"Heavy condensation in the barrels, Mr. Bentner," said Teller, seeing the Labor leader eying the glass of wine with distaste. And then Teller gave a wink of deepest meaning.

"You've been watering this stuff," cried Bentner.

"People have been watering the money too," said Teller. "What a shilling used to buy a year ago, one and sixpence won't touch now. And you know something? I'm getting afraid of what's going to happen when that next lot of money comes in." He produced a cloth and started to polish some of the glasses taken from the bar behind him.

"I'm getting sick of the mention of money," he said. "That's all that people talk about here these days. You know what all that money did, to my way of thinking? It killed interest in life. There's been many an evening here when I've listened with pleasure, while serving my customers, to three hours of good talk on shearing, wood carving, archery, gardening and—yes, treating colic in babies. It's been a treat to be among my fellow human beings. I'm not a very religious man, Mr. Bentner, but listening to talk like that, kindly and good humored, I couldn't doubt for a moment but that God Himself was right here listening with me and enjoying it just as much as me.

"And now look what's happened! The talk is money, money, money. How much is there going to be? What's going to be done with it? Who will get what? Who owes what to who? How much will go in taxes? It makes you sick. It's killed living, in my view—killed it stone dead. It's replaced it with something that isn't worth having at all.

"I'll give you a piece of plain advice, Mr. Bentner. If those Yanks offer you any more of that Gum Money, tell 'em to give it to their enemies because their friends don't deserve to be abused by it. We had a good living here and a good way of making a living. And now it's gone—or going. And money isn't any substitute for what we're losing, Mr. Bentner. No substitute at all. By God, you can't make a nation out of dollar bills and it's time the world realized that—and ourselves the first to do so."

Moved, and deep in thought, Bentner went to the dartboard, picked up the three darts and stepped back to the line. He could put a pretty dart, as the saying went, and wanted to try for the double top.

"Used to be free," said the innkeeper, busy with his glasses. "Cost a penny a dart now."

Disgusted, Bentner put the darts down and strode out.

CHAPTER VII

People learn best when taught in the terms with which they are familiar. All the lectures of Mountjoy on inflation and cheap money when put together did not have as much effect on Bentner as having to pay a penny for each dart in a dart game and eight pence for a glass of watered wine. His confidence in money as a source of prosperity and of happiness was heavily shaken by these trifling incidents. And his mind had already been made uneasy by his conversation with Davis at the bank.

In the next several days he examined the problem over and over again, at times elated by the thought that the next outpouring of Gum Money would settle everybody's financial troubles, at times made uneasy by warnings that matters would only be worse. It was, of course, easy for Mountjoy to talk of "getting rid of the money" because Mountjoy in his life had never needed for money. But Bentner had.

Bentner had known in his young days what it was to be short of a shilling. He had known the anguish which can come from the lack of a trifling sum. Money had for him an importance which lay in the fact that it was money. Pounds were pounds, dollars were dollars and shillings were shillings, and the more of these a man had, the better off he was. So he had always thought. Only painfully, slowly and with many hesitations, did he come to realize that it was possible to have a plentitude of money and still be badly off. Only by degrees did he come to realize that money was a very curious commodity, for it possessed no intrinsic value of its own. Its value depended on public confidence, which also decided whether a shilling would buy two gallons of milk or only a box of matches.

Bentner could not alone have taken the great step which the situation and Mountjoy demanded—refuse to let any more of the Gum Money come into the Duchy. He could not do this any more than a man who has once starved can throw away a loaf of bread. But he was beginning to discover that others, other than Mountjoy, were of the opinion (though often for purely emotional reasons) that the Duchy would be better off without the money.

The enthusiasm for the United States in the Duchy was beginning to wane as prices climbed and debts grew. Though it was grossly unfair, people began to attribute their misfortune to America and talk, quite without warrant, of the "money-grubbing Yanks." One sheep farmer, whose request for a loan on the wool clip had been turned down, while on a trip to Marseilles considered it his duty to throw a brick through the window of the United States Consulate there.

He was arrested by the French police and turned over to the Consulate, where he got a kindly lecture on not throwing bricks through windows and was sent away with two huge envelopes full of material about United States foreign aid to nations in need. Returning to Grand Fenwick on the bus, he read through the material carefully and, when he got home, collected all his unpaid bills and mailed them to the Consulate, asking that they be settled for him and signing his letter "Arthur Greene—the man who threw the brick through your window." By return mail he got the bills back plus another for the replacement of the glass. This demand, curiously, considerably restored American prestige in Grand Fenwick. "They're not all daft," people said on learning of the matter.

The one immediate and beneficial result of the brick throwing was that the mail service to Grand Fenwick improved immensely. Salat, the bus driver, hearing of the incident, out of gratitude became utterly punctual both in delivering and in collecting mail from the Duchy and never failed to ask the border guards to pay his respects to the fine fellow who had heaved a brick through the window of the Americans.

This being the time when news of the Gum Money earned during the past year could be expected, the improvement in the mail service relieved everybody's nerves for, of course, the whole population was awaiting the arrival of the letter, which, as a result of previous correspondence, now came from Balche and Company, of Port Elizabeth, New Jersey, finance agents for the Duchy in the United States, rather than from Bickster and Company, who merely manufactured the gum.

When the letter arrived, it was brought to the castle not by one man but by a whole delegation. It was addressed to the Count of Mountjoy, for Balche and Company were unaware that the royalties from chewing gum had brought about the collapse of the government of Grand Fenwick. Mountjoy knew perfectly well that the letter was intended for the Prime Minister, who at the time was David Bentner. But he opened it anyway without a scruple and in the presence of the delegation of some twenty or thirty people who had brought it to him and who certainly were not going to leave without some news of its contents.

The letter was very short. It consisted of but one paragraph of perhaps five lines, but out of these lines leaped a figure and the figure was $10,000,000. Grand Fenwick's share of the Gum Money this time was to be $10,000,000. Mountjoy's hand trembled as he read this figure and his mouth felt as if it had, on the moment, become full of chalk. He swallowed with difficulty and those who had crowded into his study, noticing the slight lessening of color in the Count's cheeks, sensed that there was a terrible blow coming and braced themselves to receive it.

"How much, my lord?" asked one at last.

Mountjoy, summoning the courage of his forefathers to his aid, looked steadily at the man and said, "Almost nothing. Ten thousand dollars. That is all. Sales have fallen tremendously." He thrust the letter into his pocket.

"Ten thousand dollars?" cried someone, and another said,

"We've been cheated," and another cried, "Those Yanks are keeping it for themselves." There was a little uproar of protest and of outrage, which Mountjoy allowed to continue for a while and then silenced with firm authority.

"My friends," he said, "you are actually better off. We can return now to running our own businesses without upsetting influences from abroad. But now, excuse me, I beg of you. I must pass this letter on to your Prime Minister, Mr. Bentner. He should know of this matter immediately."

When they had gone Mountjoy went from his study to his bedroom and for a while contemplated himself in a full-length mirror on the front of his wardrobe.

"Mountjoy, you dog," he said, waving a finger at his own image, "you hazard big stakes. See you play well." He then rang a little golden bell and sent his secretary to Bentner, asking whether he could call on him officially in half an hour. The secretary returned with a message that Bentner was on his way over. Mountjoy smiled. "It would be more proper if I called on him, since he is the Prime Minister," he said.

"My lord," said the secretary, "he has heard rumors that only ten thousand dollars is coming from America and he can scarcely contain himself between irritation at the amount and everybody else knowing of it before him."

Bentner was furious when he strode into the Count's study. "You," he said, pointing a stubby finger at the Count, who had risen to meet him, "are guilty of opening and of making public documents which are the concern solely of the government. You can be impeached. Impeached. And by God, I'm going to see that you are."

"Do that in public some time," said Mountjoy calmly. "You are quite effective when you demonstrate outrage. As you will see from the envelope, the letter was addressed to me and I had every right to open it."

"You knew perfectly well that it was meant for the Prime Minister, and that's me," said Bentner.

"Try proving that during impeachment proceedings," said Mountjoy. "There is nothing in our constitution, written or unwritten, that demands that a man assume that a letter addressed to himself is actually intended for another."

"As soon as you opened this letter you knew who it was for, but you let half the Duchy know its contents before passing it to me," said Bentner.

"Did I really?" asked Mountjoy quietly. "Why don't you read the letter yourself before you start making accusations?"

Bentner snatched the letter from the Count, ripped the single sheet of paper open and glanced rapidly through it. "What's this?" he cried. "You made a mistake, Mountjoy. Ten million dollars. Not ten thousand. See for yourself." He thrust the letter toward the Count, who, ignoring it, rose and went to the door to ensure that it was firmly shut.

"Really?" said Mountjoy mildly. "What a pity."

"You told them ten thousand," repeated Bentner.

"So I did."

"You made a mistake."

Mountjoy considered this for a while, meantime studying the face of Bentner, who was entirely elated by the huge sum available when he had been told there was nothing but petty cash.

"Perhaps I made a slight mistake in misreading the figure in the excitement of the moment," said Mountjoy. "But are you quite sure that you are not making a much bigger mistake in announcing the true sum? Are you quite sure, my dear Prime Minister, in whose hands rests the future of the nation, that the bigger mistake would not be to tell the people that they are now the unhappy possessors of ten million unearned dollars?

"You have seen what one million unearned dollars did to our countrymen. Ten million would do at least twice, perhaps three or four times the damage. I will not weary you with arguments whose validity you have seen demonstrated in real life. Perhaps my little slip concerning the figure—unremedied—might provide you with the solution to the problem which now faces you."

The leap from ten thousand dollars to ten million and then back to ten thousand again was too much for Bentner to take immediately. He boggled, his mind lumbering around here and there like a bull controlled by a skillful matador in the person of Mountjoy.

"You are still free to act in whatever manner you think the best," said Mountjoy. "Far be it from me to usurp the privileges and indeed the duties of the Prime Minister. But, with a sense of duty to my country and with a desire to be of service to you in these particularly arduous circumstances, I have provided you with a choice among alternatives.

"Those alternatives are these. You can officially confirm the news that only ten thousand dollars has been received this year, which will make any public division of the money impossible for the whole amount will be swallowed in paying only a part of the national debt—a gift of your party to the nation, I might add.

"Or you can take the other alternative. You can say that I made a mistake or that I lied. You can announce the doleful news that the Duchy now has ten million dollars, that the national debt can be paid at one swoop and that everybody can expect to receive—after payment of taxes—well over the equivalent of several years' wages. In which case you will have unending problems of which you have seen the beginning already."

"Ten million dollars," whispered Bentner in agony. "Ten million dollars. It's more than we'll see in the Duchy in ten years' time. How can anyone turn down ten million dollars?"

"Not everyone can," said Mountjoy smoothly. "Only those who, like myself, being accustomed to money, have perhaps less attachment to it. Which is why I decided to make it easy for you. The people couldn't have turned it down. But they are not now expecting more than ten thousand. And you yourself—my dear Bentner—I do appreciate your difficulties. I know how hard it must be for a man from a working-class family to turn his back on a fortune.

"Money has been your master for so long that you have to jig at its bidding. It is not the nobility, of course, who are enemies of the working class, though working-class prejudices have always been directed against their betters. No, money is the enemy of the workingman, as I am sure you now appreciate. And so, in the name of the workingman whom you represent, I call on you to turn your back on the enemy of your class and have nothing to do with this ruinous treasure."

"I don't know that I can do it," said Bentner. "I don't know that I've got it in me."

"You are not without aid," said Mountjoy. "You can either pray or resign."

It was the thought of resignation—not prayer—that provided the turning point. "Resign?" echoed Bentner. "And throw away the greatest majority my party ever had? Never."

"Then I recommend that you go down on your knees and ask Our Maker, in the national interest, to give you the strength of character to turn away from ten million dollars."

But the thought of resignation and the ruin of his party had stiffened Bentner's resolve. "I'll tell them ten thousand and not a penny more," he said.

"Bravo," cried Mountjoy. "I begin to believe, listening to you, that when the aristocracy have finally disappeared from the earth, there may be enough men of character among the common people for civilization to continue."

"I was wondering, however," said Bentner slowly, "whether, without anyone being a whit the wiser, we couldn't take a little for ourselves—I have a few commitments. Mountjoy's icy stare silenced him. He shrugged a little and said, "All right. Can't hang a fellow for trying, can you?"

CHAPTER VIII

Both Mountjoy and Bentner, being now firmly of the opinion that the public should not be told the correct amount of the Gum Money, so recommended to Gloriana at a meeting of the Privy Council. To their dismay, Gloriana thought otherwise.

"You two must remember that this is a democracy," she said. "You cannot impose your plans on the public by subterfuge, without destroying our democracy. That democracy is more valuable than the dollars you wish to hide."

"My dear sovereign lady," said Mountjoy, "even in a democracy a government must keep from the people certain secrets which, if published, would do untold harm because of the emotional reaction—unconnected with rational thinking—which they would generate. Governments, even democratic governments, must protect the people from themselves."

"Quite right, Ma'am," said Bentner. "Tell the people about this and they would go hog-wild. Why, they'd be ordering automobiles and demanding that we put in petrol stations and widen the roads. There'd be a surge of traffic deaths and accidents. We'd have to increase the police force, start fining our own people for speeding, set up courts to try cases. No end of trouble, Ma'am. Best say nothing about it, but just quietly get rid of the money some way."

"And what about next year and the year after?" asked Gloriana. "Remember we are required to keep this chewing gum franchise in operation nine more years. Do you think it right to lie each year to the people about the earnings? And when the people find out—as they are bound to—that they have not only been lied to but what they regard as their legitimate dividends have been given away without their being consulted—what then? How would either of you two gentlemen be able to lead a party, let alone form a government, after an exposure like that?"

With such arguments Gloriana persuaded her Prime Minister and the leader of her Loyal Opposition that the real amount of the dollar earnings must officially be announced to the people through the Council of Freemen. "Do not distrust our people," she said. "They are perhaps wiser than you give them credit for."

Bentner made the announcement. He passed over the original statement of the Count's that the amount was but ten thousand dollars and said that there were ten million dollars and he had every reason to believe that the royalties would amount to the equivalent of that sum, or more, in the years ahead.

Immediately such a storm erupted in the chamber that Bentner was quite drowned out and the Speaker, up on his feet in a moment and hammering with his gavel to restore silence, could not be heard either. The roar was like that of a football crowd at the scoring of an unexpected goal. Papers were flung into the air. Members embraced each other, two or three performed a kind of jig on the benches and it took the sergeant-at-arms and four of his men a quarter of an hour before the Speaker could make himself heard.

"I must warn honorable members," he thundered, when at last his voice could be distinguished above the hubbub, "that I have the power to suspend them for unbecoming behavior, and I will use that power if there is a repetition of this kind of demonstration."

The members sat down and the Speaker turned to Bentner. "The Honorable Prime Minister has just informed the House that the sum of ten million dollars American was to be paid into the Duchy's Treasury from the sales of chewing gum," he said. "The Prime Minister has the floor and will proceed."

Bentner licked his lips. What he had to say now was going to provide the members with an even greater shock. Summoning up his courage, he plunged on. He reminded the chamber of the disasters which had followed the previous disbursement of the Gum Money. He spoke of the inflation of the national currency, the increased public and private debt, the rise in rents, in prices and in wages.

"I have now to tell the House," he said, "that I must reverse the stand which I took when the first large amount of American money reached us. At that time I demanded that it be shared among the people. I now propose—and I will fight for this proposal whatever the cost to myself and my party—that we turn our back upon this new sum, that we refuse to allow it to interfere with our economy, to sabotage our wages, our prices and the values of our products. In short I propose that we devise some plan for dumping these millions in some place where they can do us no hurt."

The uproar that had followed the announcement of the true sum had its counterpart now in the paralyzed silence of shock and of disbelief that settled upon the House. In that silence not a sound was heard but the buzzing of a fly on a windowpane. In that silence Mountjoy, getting the Speaker's eye, rose to present the Opposition point of view. That view, he stressed, coincided exactly with the stand taken by the government. Government and Opposition were in complete agreement regarding the disposition of the funds.

"In times of national crisis," Mountjoy said, "it is a tradition that all parties join hands. Such a crisis confronts us now. I pledge full support and that of my party to the Prime Minister and his government."

It was then that the dam burst again. This time there was no dancing on the benches, but members were on their feet in a moment, shaking their fists at Mountjoy and Bentner, and again drowning out the Speaker in the uproar. Three were ejected by the sergeant-at-arms before order was restored and Bentner could go over once again his reasons for deciding that the money must not be allowed into the Duchy. Actually all were, from their own experience, aware of the reasons. They were now suffering in public the agony which Bentner had suffered in private—the anguish of parting with ten million dollars, which experience told them must be done, but which training and emotion made extremely difficult.

Avoiding the decision for a while, they fumed at Mountjoy and demanded to know why he had originally given out the news that only ten thousand dollars was available.

"I disguised the sum thinking that if the full figure were published, people would not have the courage or the wisdom to turn it back," said Mountjoy. "I wanted to spare you the agony you now endure and the Duchy the peril in which it now stands. I trust I misjudged you and my fellow citizens and that you and the people will have the courage to turn down these ten million dollars which menace our whole future—these and the millions more which are undoubtedly to follow."

He got no immediate assurance on this point and the debate which followed was long and the questions asked searching.

"Why could not the money be just left in America at interest?" one member asked.

"That could be done," Bentner replied, "but it would merely postpone the decision. The money would keep increasing until not ten million but perhaps a hundred million dollars lay to the credit of the Duchy. Who among us could turn his back on such a fortune? No, the longer we delay, the harder the decision will be.

"What lies at the basis of all this," he went on, "is whether we want to continue with the kind of life we have lived in the past or whether we want to change it completely so that our children will depend for their security and happiness not on their work but on unearned wealth coming in from abroad. Do we want our descendants to be self-supporting or to become a nation of wealthy idlers? Putting all the figures aside, that is the question you have to ask yourselves."

"What about the debts already incurred?" asked another. "They were contracted in the belief that there would be money coming to pay them."

"Why not keep enough of the money to pay off all the debts of individuals and the government and abolish taxation for the rest of this year?" another asked.

Nobody wanted to keep all the money. Nobody advocated taking it and dividing it up among the voters of Grand Fenwick. Everybody agreed, in varying degrees, that the money should not be allowed to disturb the economy of Grand Fenwick—the delicate relationship of labor to produce to wage which had been achieved through the years.

In the end it was agreed, thirty-three to seven, that all public and private debts arising from the previous disbursement of dollars should be paid off with the new money. Thereafter not a dollar of it was to be allowed to enter the country.

The seven who voted against this wanted sufficient of the funds placed in the Treasury to make it unnecessary for anyone in Grand Fenwick to pay taxes for several years to come. This was opposed by Mountjoy, who pointed out again that if people do not pay taxes they lose interest in their government. "For a government to remain healthy," he argued, "every penny of a nation's budget should be subject to scrutiny and debate. This will never be so if the money is not contributed in the first place by the voters themselves."

After the vote a motion was made from the floor that the problem of disposing of the unneeded millions of dollars be turned over "to our gracious and sovereign Lady the Duchess Gloriana the Twelfth, who may call for advice in this matter from her humble privy councilors." This was passed without dissent, for the people would gladly give to their Duchess, who was above politics, that trust which they withheld from Mountjoy and Bentner.

Gloriana had very little experience in money matters and was not regarded by her consort, Tully Bascomb, as a practical handler of finance. She tended, like many other women, to get hold of a principle which applied in a limited situation and, willy-nilly, to apply it in every situation. She went on occasional shopping expeditions to Villeurbanne or Lyons or Marseilles and bought large quantities of things for which she had no real need because they were cheap. Tully was quite incapable of convincing her that nothing is cheap if it isn't needed. She also tended to buy against future needs which did not eventuate. These, of course, were but peccadilloes common to many, but Tully was at best disturbed that his wife should be entrusted now with the problem of getting rid of close to ten million dollars.

"And yet," he mused, "perhaps she is just the person to do the job. She has been able to get rid of every penny of her personal allowance as it comes to her."

Gloriana had heard all she wanted to hear on the subject of money from Bentner and Mountjoy. Seeking a fresh viewpoint, she went to see Dr. Kokintz. The great mathematician and physicist had been quite unperturbed by the recent financial turmoil, though his days had been enlivened by an occasional call to repair a television set.

"Are you sure there isn't something really expensive that I can buy you?" she asked. "You're not interested in astronomy? We could build you a nice big observatory, with a huge telescope." But Kokintz said that his interest in astronomy did not justify such a vast expenditure. He did want one piece of equipment, however, which would have to be specially made and might prove expensive.

"What is it?" asked Gloriana eagerly.

"Two pieces of case-hardened steel with the surfaces optically ground to a given curve," said Kokintz. "I think only Calton Research Supply in Scranton, Pennsylvania, could make up what is needed."

"Order them right away," said Gloriana. "Tell them to ship them out by special airplane. Don't let them spare any cost whatever. How much do you think they'll come to?"

"Perhaps two hundred dollars each," said Kokintz. "But the special plane might cost several thousands of dollars."

"Oh blow," said Gloriana. "Can't you think of anything better than that?" But Kokintz couldn't. She asked him what he was working on, hoping for some ideas. He replied that he was busy with two problems. One was an old one—the affinity of most elements for oxygen. All science accepted but none understood it. He suspected that somewhere in the relationship between oxygen and other elements there was a key to the problem of the transmutation of one element into another.

A second line of investigation which also occupied him was ultra-high-frequency vibrations. "We have developed already an airplane that will travel faster than sound," he said. "And yet I suspect that it will be possible to develop a sound that will travel faster than an airplane."

"What earthly use will that be?" asked Gloriana.

Kokintz removed his thick-lensed glasses and, failing to find anything else immediately, pulled out the tail of his shirt and polished the lenses with it. "It may have no use at all," he said. "But then, use is only one measure of value. Knowledge has its own value. Adding to knowledge makes man more wholly man." Gloriana left, having made a mental note to buy Dr. Kokintz several cases of tissues with which to clean his spectacles.

Then one day, quite by happenstance, she discovered what to do with the unwanted millions. She had been studying the *Times* and in utter boredom had turned to the financial pages. An article at the beginning of the section detailed a decline in the value of industrials and a slight rise in rails and the value of government bonds.

"Why didn't I think of that before?" she demanded. "People lose millions on the stock market without the slightest effort every day. I'll just buy shares and keep on buying them and I'm bound to lose every penny. And it will be fun too."

She reflected for a moment that not everybody lost money on the stock exchange. Some people—vague distant people whom one never met—made money on the stock exchange. Some people (especially gifted in financial matters) even got their whole income from investments in the stock market. But these, she was sure, were people who made the most careful study of the value of stocks, of the condition of particular industries, of the management and research programs of the companies in which they were interested. And even so, they sometimes lost.

Encouraged by these reflections, she spread the financial page of the *Times* carefully on a table before her. Then she shut her eyes tight and stuck a pin in the page. The pin pierced the page opposite the name Westwood Coal and Carriage.

That same day an airmail letter was dispatched from Grand Fenwick, over the signature of Her Grace Gloriana XII, to Balche and Company, of New Jersey, the Duchy's financial agents in the United States, telling them to invest six million dollars in the stock of that unsuspecting corporation.

CHAPTER IX

The Westwood Coal and Carriage Company was a surprising survivor of the American transportation boom which had followed on the heels of the Civil War. The company had been founded in the middle of that conflict, having undertaken to transport supplies to McClellan's army for a fee which somewhat detracted from the patriotism of the service. The company had started with drovers and wagons and had, with the earnings gained, branched after the war into rolling stock. An interest in railroad engines had naturally led to an interest in coal mines which provided the fuel for the engines.

At the beginning of the twentieth century, Westwood Coal and Carriage Company was a force to be reckoned with in both transportation and mining. But about then there had been a shift in transportation techniques, which the company's directors (Ted and Cy Westwood, sons of General Hiram Westwood, the company's founder) had not been sufficiently astute to gauge.

A few automobiles started chuffing around the roads powered

some by steam and some by a derivative of the rock oil called petroleum, the first great wells of which had been discovered just before the Civil War in Pennsylvania. Ted and Cy Westwood shouldered these developments aside as mere toys in the world of transportation. Automobiles, which they pictured as self-service trains, would never, they thought, get anywhere because roads throughout the nation were uncommonly bad. And it was plain that the more these roads were used, the worse they would become. Who then would want to be bumped along at five to eight miles an hour in an automobile when they could ride at fifty miles an hour on a smooth roadbed of steel rails?

And electricity would plainly never replace coal as a fuel because it just didn't have the muscle. It was all right for producing a wavering glow in light bulbs or for powering telephones. But it would never turn machines; and since it had to be conducted along wires in any case, the nation must become a horrible tangle of wires, a sort of netting of wiring, for electricity to have any universal use. Therefore rails and coal were sound and no change in company activity, it was thought, was called for.

But over the years, what with reduced demand for coal, the increases in the wages of coal miners and the depletion of the deposits, the mines of Westwood Coal and Carriage Company proved less and less profitable and were sold one by one until but two remained to the company. And the company's holdings in railroad rights of way and rolling stock were also reduced as freight and passengers went increasingly by road, until the company decided to get out of the railroad business altogether. Too late the aging directors turned to automobile manufacture.

There were, to be sure, some initial profits from the Westwood motorcar, but the real profits from automobiles now lay in mass production and the Westwood car, a late arrival in the market, was almost hand-built. Each year the directors of the company had to make a big loan from the bank to finance the production of their new model. Each year they just managed to pay the loan off. The company was starved for capital and had shown no profit for ten years. For seven of those years it had been run at a book loss.

And yet, with suicidal fidelity, Westwood Coal and Carriage Company continued to operate in those fields where past experience had proved that it could not succeed—transportation and coal. At its factory in western Michigan it turned out six thousand cars a year. And each year the board announced that if the six thousand could only be increased to sixty thousand, there would be a handsome profit to share (in part) with the faithful stockholders.

This was the situation of the Westwood Coal and Carriage Company when Balche and Company of New Jersey was surprised by instructions from Gloriana to invest six million dollars of the Duchy's earnings in shares. The letter came to Mr. Joseph Balche himself, a large man of great dignity, whose white handlebar moustache suggested he was a survivor of McKinley's Cabinet.

"Westwood Coal and Carriage," he said on reading the letter. "Six million dollars? Upon my word."

He reached for his *Financial Times*, wondered whether some

miracle had occurred of which he was ignorant and looked up the quotation on Westwood Coal. It was two and seven-eighths, down an eighth. He glanced at the letter again to make sure he had read it correctly. There was no mistake.

When under great stress Mr. Balche watered his geraniums. They grew in a box outside the window of his office and he had a watering can on the floor of the bathroom adjoining for this purpose. He went into the bathroom, got the watering can, opened the window and started watering. He watched the neat jets of water from the rose on the can splash on the leaves of the geraniums and cascade in silvery waterfalls into the black loam of the box. The sight soothed him. His nerve was steadied and he returned to his desk and without a further glance at the letter called up John Dibbs of the brokerage firm of Dibbs, Hedstrom, Morris, Strong, Williams and Benjamin on Wall Street.

John Dibbs was of a character completely the opposite of Mr. Joseph Balche, and the two, though they had had many business dealings, had never met. Dibbs had a large stomach, a red face and meaty shoulders and smoked cigars. He used his desk quite often as a place on which to rest his feet. He seemed to have received his training in business behavior from watching early movies dealing with gangsters and newspapermen. His manner was that of Chicago in the days of snap-brim hats and submachine guns. "Dibbs," he said into the mouthpiece of the telephone. "What can I do for you?"

"Joseph Balche here," said the other. "I have a client who is interested in Westwood Coal and Carriage. What is available?"

"Available?" asked Dibbs. "I should think everything the company has is available, including the president's wife. Two and five-eighths."

"Down a quarter since yesterday," said Balche, ignoring the crudity of the other's humor. "See what you can do about rounding up everything that is offered. My client is interested in acquiring the largest possible holdings."

"Who is your client?" asked Dibbs.

"At this point I would prefer not to say," said Balche somewhat distantly.

"Okay. Answer me this question. Is this new money?" "Yes," said Mr. Balche, "it is. My client has not previously invested in the stock market."

"Well," said Dibbs, "if you want to cure them of investing forevermore—and I personally would regard that as a favor because this new money coming into the market starts too many hares running across the fields for the serious investor—go ahead and make the purchases. But if you want your client to continue with an interest in the stock market, then I would advise mutual funds or something more solid. Because Westwood Coal is going nowhere else but down and your client is going to lose seventy cents on every dollar."

"Thank you for your advice," said Balche icily. "Meanwhile will you kindly go ahead with buying up all the shares available, at whatever price is in keeping with current values."

"What's your limit?" asked Dibbs.

"Six million dollars," said Mr. Balche and hung up.

Mr. Dibbs had no geraniums to water. He glanced at the clock and noted that it was four in the afternoon and the Stock Exchange was therefore closed. He struggled into his overcoat and, ignoring the elevator, scuttled down the four flights of rickety stairs in which his brokerage company was located and out into Wall Street. He turned sharply to the right, made his way past J. P. Morgan's solemn bank, entered the swinging doors of a saloon nearby and, crossing the floor strewn with sawdust, ordered a manhattan.

He was fortunate in that Hans, the German proprietor and head bartender, was on duty, for when the Stock Exchange closed, Hans was the only really reliable and central source of information on the whole street. Hans knew every one of the several hundred rumors which flitted up and down the street every day. He not only knew the rumors but he knew the sources, knew who repeated them, knew to whom they were repeated, knew who believed them and who disbelieved them.

And out of all this knowledge could be distilled the degree of truth in each one of the stories of mergers, or recapitalization, of mortgage and of tax proceedings which flitted around the little village of Wall Street during each short but vigorous day.

That Mr. Dibbs was able to get to the bar at all in that crowded saloon was attributable to the fact that brokers had, by custom, places at the bar as they had booths on the floor of the Stock Exchange. As soon as he entered, it was known that he would require a slot and so room was made for him.

Hans, of course, did not bring him his drink. Hans had been known to serve only one drink in thirty years and that was to a former President of the United States who had been brought to Hans's Bar after a tour of the Stock Exchange. Then Hans had himself reached for the bottle of bourbon, unerringly selecting the right brand, and decanted a drink of just the right size for the former President, with the solemnity of a cardinal giving communion to a bishop.

Jimmy, the Irish bartender, brought Mr. Dibbs his manhattan, and Dibbs, first eating the cherry as he always did, then took a good pull at his drink and, listening to the buzz of talk about him with an occasional and unexpected laugh here and there, reflected that in the face of six million dollars available for investment in Westwood Coal and Carriage, nothing in the world made any sense anyway. He was asked a few questions by his neighbors and answered them without any reflection whatever, scarcely conscious of what he was saying, so bowled over was he with the order to invest six million dollars in worthless stock. And then Hans—tall Hans with his face like that of a Knight Templar carved upon a tomb, his ginger hair mixed with white and his pale-blue eyes, which seemed incapable of a sparkle of either excitement or grief—noted that John Dibbs was preoccupied and had therefore something on his mind.

Hans always took up his station in the center of the bar, leaning against the back bar and greeting nobody. Yet he managed to bend his head down close to each of his old customers and exchange a secret word before the customer left, and he was particularly astute at noticing anything amiss in the behavior of his clients which indicated either that his client needed information or had information to impart.

So seeing Dibbs not his ebullient and somewhat coarse self, but drinking his manhattan as if it were water (he had two in five minutes) and neglecting to light the end of a new cigar, Hans moved slowly, almost imperceptibly, toward him and bent his head down so that his ear was close to Dibbs's mouth.

"Westwood Coal?" whispered Dibbs.

Hans straightened up slowly and gave only the slightest shake of his Knight Templar's head. Then without a further sign he returned to his station in the center of the bar, watching for others of his customers in distress.

That scarcely seen shake of the head had conveyed to Dibbs the information he needed—namely that no rumors concerning Westwood Coal were abroad on Wall Street. That meant that nothing whatever out of the ordinary was happening at the company—either actual or speculative. And so Dibbs was left to ruminate over the problem of why someone would want to buy Westwood Coal and was prepared to spend six million dollars in so doing.

This puzzle he must solve, though strictly it was none of his business. But he had to know whether the purchase was being made out of pure ignorance or out of inside knowledge or some deep and subtle plan which would result in Westwood Coal becoming in the next few days or weeks a valuable asset instead of remaining a complete turkey. So he ordered one more manhattan and signified to

Jimmy the bartender that that was to be the last by paying for them all. And when the drink arrived he was calm enough to light his cigar and examine the problem with more detachment.

The first conclusion he reached was that six million dollars wasn't fool's money. It was too big a sum to be in the hands of an idiot. Therefore whoever was going to invest it knew something. The something he knew was unknown to the rest of Wall Street or Hans would have heard of it—however secret. Therefore that something was the secret of the investor alone. It was something he himself was perhaps going to do with Westwood Coal and which he had discussed with nobody.

"What?" That was the question.

The company had no assets—or rather what it had were pledged and overpledged to banks in return for loans. In fact, the company's assets were in such a poor way that it was public knowledge that the banks were thinking of foreclosing on the two remaining coal mines in the company's hands, on its tiny automobile factory in western Michigan and on its remaining forty-three miles of railroad—long ago leased to the Long Island Central, which itself couldn't make any money.

Government contract, maybe? Had someone in the company managed to get a government contract, perhaps in connection with the space program, which would make it worth while for someone else to buy up the whole business? The three manhattans glowing within him, it seemed to Mr. Dibbs that this was the only possibility. Some big lump of business was coming to Westwood Coal and

Carriage. This survivor from the age of the dinosaurs was at last going to get a bundle of hay.

Jimmy, the young bartender, picked up the five-dollar bill that Dibbs had put on the bar for his drinks and inquired jokingly, "What should I put my life savings into, Mr. Dibbs?"

"Westwood Coal and Carriage," said Dibbs. And those who heard looked at first surprised and then thoughtful.

CHAPTER X

The six million dollars which Gloriana, acting on a decision made by a pin, had invested in Westwood Coal and Carriage readily purchased the majority of the shares of that company so that it was now owned, almost entirely, by the Duchy of Grand Fenwick. Nor was the full six million required to obtain control of the company for the Duchy, actually for the Duchess. Almost two and a half million dollars was left over, and Mr. Joseph Balche considered sending a cable to the Duchy asking for further instructions regarding the investment of this amount. On reflection he decided against this. There was no cable office in Grand Fenwick. That much he knew.

A cable to the Duchy would be transmitted to Paris, retransmitted probably to Marseilles, and then mailed to Grand Fenwick since there was no telephone system in the Duchy connecting the little nation with the outside world. Mountjoy had been able to obtain the installation of a telephone system about the castle and from the castle to the frontier guard, but there were no outside lines, for the reason that before the arrival of the Gum Money, the Duchy was not able to afford long-distance calls. Mr. Balche reflected that in these days of jet-propelled airplanes, an airmail letter went as fast almost as a cable and, in the case of the Duchy, would probably arrive earlier. Also the Duchess had herself sent her original instructions to buy by surface mail, indicating strongly that no great haste was required.

In his letter Mr. Balche stated that he had been able to acquire for the Duchy 71 percent of the shares of Westwood Coal and Carriage and that the Duchy could therefore dictate the future policy of the company and secure the election of a new board of directors. He warned that the company's affairs were in the worst possible way and added that he had thought it proper to require a full audit of the company's business and this would be sent to Her Grace at the earliest moment.

"Since the purchase of these shares for Your Grace they have fallen in value from two and an eighth to one and a quarter," the letter continued. "I had hoped that when news of the purchase got about, it would bring about a rise in the market value of the shares, but the company's financial record proved too formidable an obstacle to such a rally.

"Regarding the balance of close to two and a half million dollars, I would suggest that this be invested in County of Tokyo Bonds, which are safe and which carry a remarkable interest rate of 8 percent."

Gloriana was a little annoyed when she got this letter. She

didn't expect to have any money left over. She wanted it all spent on the worthless shares and wrote to Mr. Balche instructing him to do this. "I don't care how much you pay for the shares," she wrote, "but you are to use up all the money buying them. When you write to me again, I hope it will be to report that not a penny of the six million dollars remains uninvested."

The remaining shares were largely in the hands of the directors of the company. Mr. Balche considered how best to get possession of them and decided this time not to go through Dibbs but to approach the directors himself. He believed that the Duchy was about to suffer a huge financial loss, and he felt that by getting the shares as cheaply as possible, he ought to both reduce the loss and spread it over as much paper as he could.

A man of much dignity and a quiet mind, he was able, very largely with a good number of telephone calls, to round up a good many of the remaining shares, though he had to pay higher than for those in the hands of the small holders. The price of the shares then started to go up. A rumor about a space contract, connected with the buying of Westwood Coal, flitted around Wall Street, stimulated by the buying of the shares and Mr. Dibbs's advice on investment to Jimmy in Hans's Bar, which had been overheard by several brokers.

They went up an eighth, then a quarter and then a surprising one and an eighth. The buzz in Wall Street spread to Washington, to San Francisco, Los Angeles and Chicago. Government contracts let out were pored through and inquiries were made at the National Aeronautics and Space Agency concerning the rumor of a fat contract for Westwood Coal. Other speculative money came in looking for Westwood Coal shares. In two weeks the price of the shares had doubled, entirely on their demand value, and at the end of that time John Dibbs called Mr. Balche from his Wall Street office.

"About Westwood Coal," he said. "I have a client here who would like to meet your client and discuss a deal."

"Impossible," said Mr. Balche. "My client is not even in this country."

"Who is your client?" asked Dibbs.

"I am not at liberty to say."

"Look," said Dibbs, "this whole thing is a soap bubble. You know it and I know it. Your client is trying to bid up the price of the shares and the game is just about over. I've had inquiries made at every government office and all along the line and there's no new business and no new financing coming to Westwood Coal. This kind of gambling is bad for Wall Street and bad for business. So why doesn't your client just get together with mine and at least discuss intentions? Maybe when the whole thing blows up something could be saved."

"Tell me," said Mr. Balche, eying the geraniums glowing red in the window box, "is your client interested in buying the shares held by my client?"

"No," said Dibbs. "He owns the remaining shares and he wants to know what's the action."

"The action is that I have a certain sum of money and no more with which to buy the outstanding shares in Westwood Coal," said

Balche. "Your client can either sell them or take his chances on the shares devaluing because there is no more money looking for these shares and nothing available beyond the sum at my disposal."

"How much is at your disposal?" asked Dibbs.

"I am not going to mention a figure, but it is limited," said Balche. "You might inform your client that if he is not willing to sell now while he can get a good price, my client will start disposing of shares in large blocks about the middle of next week. At that time the price should go down rapidly, and when your client decides to sell, he won't get what he could get now."

"That sounds suspiciously like a threat," said Dibbs.

"It is a threat," said Mr. Balche smoothly. "And a very serious one. I am glad you recognize it."

"Your client must be out of his head," said Dibbs. "I've had a six-alarm check run on that company and it has no assets whatever, tangible or intangible. Do you realize that its average bank account has never exceeded thirty thousand dollars for the past eighty years?"

"A very small sum indeed," said Mr. Balche. "Will you kindly call me back if your client decides to sell?" He put down the telephone and considered the remarkably small bank account of Westwood Coal. It was not, he decided, surprising in a company which had showed only losses for so long and had been kept alive on borrowed funds.

The following day Dibbs called again to say that his client had agreed to sell the remaining shares at four and a quarter to Mr. Balche. Obedient to his instructions, Mr. Balche bought them on behalf of Gloriana, and wrote her a letter saying that she now possessed all the shares of that company and no cash, for the whole six million dollars was gone. The directors, he added, had been instructed to continue their business as usual pending an audit of the company's assets, which was still being made.

In the week that followed, there being no more bidding for shares, and with no news of new products planned or new contracts received, the value of the shares started to decline. In the second week after completing the purchase Gloriana, reading the *London Times*, which was a few days out of date, and figuring with a pencil, was able to congratulate herself on having lost three-quarters of a million dollars. The second week things leveled out a bit and she lost only half a million.

The third week a prolonged oil-refinery strike was settled, and in the glow of happiness which always touches Wall Street on these joyous occasions, stocks advanced sharply and Westwood Coal was, almost as an act of generosity, included in the advance. Six hundred thousand dollars of the previous losses were wiped out. But then, two days later, realizing with horror what it had done, Wall Street recovered its senses in so far as Westwood Coal was concerned and the price of shares dropped one and a quarter, so that Gloriana, after only four weeks as owner of the company, could claim to have successfully lost four and a half million dollars.

She felt very proud of herself. Not many people, she was sure, could get rid of four and a half million dollars in just four weeks without working very hard at it. And she had scarcely worked at all.

She had written a couple of letters and glanced at the financial columns of the *London Times*. That was all.

To lose a million dollars a week with such little energy, she reflected, took a particular kind of genius, and she was so pleased about it all that she was about to tell both her husband Tully and the Count of Mountjoy, now leader of her Loyal Opposition but still her devoted guardian, when she got another airmail letter from Balche and Company.

The envelope was very fat, stuffed with papers, and caused considerable comment as it was brought from the frontier postbox to the castle. In fact, it was passed into several people's hands for examination on the way. All felt the thickness of it and admired the stamps and speculated on the news which it contained and which they were sure vitally affected them.

And so it did. The thickness of the letter was accounted for by the fact that it contained a fifty-page audit of the assets of Westwood Coal. The inventory was astonishingly precise with a value allotted to each item, ranging all the way from cylinder blocks to paper clips and typewriters. Gloriana riffled through these pages, feeling slightly concerned because all that material which now belonged to the Duchy represented a vast and untidy lump of responsibility.

The front page, she found, struck a balance between assets and liabilities. Gloriana skipped that because she had come to doubt the accuracy of company balance sheets. They always agreed down to the very last penny and that, she knew, was purest fiction. Nobody could make anything come out to a penny. Supposing just as the company had balanced its books the janitor, sweeping up, found a sixpence on the floor—what then? Wouldn't that unbalance the whole thing?

She turned to the letter from Mr. Balche. It was a formal letter, striving to be cold and impersonal. And yet there was a touch of almost triumph and congratulation in the introductory paragraphs, which was explained in paragraph three. Paragraph three read:

> As Your Grace will see on examining the audit, the auditors discovered that for many years Westwood Coal has been operating on a cash basis and the amount of cash in the company's hands—ten million dollars—far exceeds the price paid by Your Grace for ownership of the company. Your Grace will forgive me expressing my pleasure at so adroit a stroke of business by one thought unversed in financial affairs.
>
> I must confess that I myself was surprised by your order to purchase these shares, which have brought a profit in cash of four million dollars and have acquired for Your Grace the other assets of the company. These assets, to be sure, consist for the most part of certain mortgaged buildings, goodwill, etc., of this fine old firm. I have taken the liberty of getting the advice of an automotive production engineer on the inventory of the automobile factory in western Michigan. He has assured me that there are enough parts available to make 100 Westwood automobiles of the 1928 model which could be sold on the antique car market at six thousand dollars apiece and the net profit here, without looking further, would be in the

neighborhood of a further quarter of a million dollars.

I await with respect Your Grace's further instructions.

Yours truly,

Joseph Balche

CHAPTER XI

Gloriana was so vexed at having made four million dollars when she had firmly intended to lose six millions that for a while she refused even to think about money and would not write to Mr. Balche. She felt that he was in some obscure way responsible for the failure of her plan to lose on the stock market. She felt he should have known that hidden around in safes, and drawers, and cashboxes of Westwood Coal was ten million dollars in cash. But at the end of a week she convinced herself that she had been the victim of a stroke of fortune—the well-known "beginner's luck" which awaited all who ventured into a new field. She consoled herself with the thought that she had only to persevere and continue to invest her money in the stock market and she would lose everything.

She got a little oblique support for this view from Mountjoy, who often came to her apartments for tea, sometimes with Tully and sometimes alone, for Gloriana was as devoted to him as if he were her father.

"Bobo," she said to him at one of these tea sessions, "what are shares? When people talk about buying shares, what are they talking about?"

"They are talking about buying shares of stock in a company," said Mountjoy, sniffing delicately at the aroma of the tea in his cup. Darjeeling, he decided, and after another sniff, December crop. This being the best time of the year for Darjeeling teas, he added only a small amount of sugar to his cup so as not to destroy the exquisite flavor of the infusion.

"Five minutes is about best, depending on the water," he said aloud, taking a sip. "In fact, I would say five minutes is perfection."

"Five minutes for what?" asked Gloriana.

"Allowing the Darjeeling to stand before pouring," said Mountjoy. "The chemists, of course, say three minutes, but they are concerned only with the tannin and caffeine content. This is excellent."

"Thank you, Bobo," said Gloriana, and she was really pleased, for the Count viewed tea in the same light in which he viewed wine and often remarked that between the two there was at least a collateral relationship.

"You had mentioned stocks, Your Grace," said Mountjoy. "Oh yes," said Gloriana. "I suppose in my position I really ought to know something about these things. But I don't know what is a stock and what is a share and what is a bond or whether they are indeed all the same things."

"Stocks and shares are the same thing," said Mountjoy. "If you own stocks you own part of a company, and of course if you own all the stock you own the whole company. You share in the fortunes of the company—its profits and its losses. And this being so, you have the right to participate in the election of the managers of the company."

"I always thought that the president and the board of directors owned the company," said Gloriana.

"Oh no, Your Grace," said Mountjoy. "No more than the Prime Ministers and elected representatives of any nation own the nation. They are only officials—servants. Though they may themselves own shares in the company concerned which could make them part owners as well."

"And what about bonds?" asked Gloriana. "What are they?"

"A bond gives no ownership at all," said Mountjoy. "It is a loan to a company—or a government—which has to be repaid by the end of a certain time at its face value. Meanwhile interest must be paid on the bond at a rate which is fixed. Bonds are safer than stocks because the interest is guaranteed and the money paid for the bond must be returned at the end of the period. But the return from bonds is not very high and in some cases it is not even high enough to offset the devaluation of the money paid for the bond."

"So bonds are safer than stocks—for investing."

"Yes, indeed," said Mountjoy. "And of stocks, preferred stocks are safer than common stocks."

"What are they?" asked the Duchess.

"Stocks which also carry a fixed rate of return. They are not a loan of money to the company concerned but an investment of money in the company. However, the amount of profit shared among preferred stockholders is limited to a certain figure, and to compensate for this, they get their money before any profit is divided among the holders of common stocks."

"So the most risky stocks of all are common stocks?"

"Quite so," said Mountjoy. "Investing in common stocks without specialized knowledge is a form of gambling. And, as you know, only professional gamblers win and sometimes even they lose."

"Thank you, Bobo," said Gloriana. "Do have one of the *millefeuilles*. They're delicious. I got them at the little bakery by the market cross in Villeurbanne."

It did not occur to Mountjoy, although of an astute mind, that he had been questioned about stocks and bonds by Gloriana because the Duchess had decided to get rid of the surplus millions by investing them in the stock market. Patterns of thinking, developed during the course of his lifetime, prevented him from reaching such a conclusion.

One pattern, firmly established, was that people invested in the stock market to make money. The contrary concept of investing in stocks in order to lose money never entered his mind. Again, although he knew that Gloriana herself had been made responsible by the people of Grand Fenwick for "getting rid" of the Gum Money, Mountjoy saw in this merely a neutralization of the money—the removing of the fortune out of the politics and economics of the

Duchy by placing it in the care and charge of the Duchess, who was above all political considerations.

Handing the money over to the Duchess, he reflected, had the effect of neutralizing it, and he was a little chagrined that he had not thought of this solution himself, for in his father's time there had been a brilliant precedent for this resort to royalty in the resolution of an enormous financial problem. The problem was that of the disposal of the Cullinan diamond—a diamond of the first water and as big as a man's fist. Broken into small stones and sold, it would enormously depreciate the price of diamonds throughout the world. Retained in one stone, there was simply not enough money at current values available for any individual to buy it.

The problem of getting rid of the diamond without hurting world diamond prices and production had been neatly solved by giving the stone outright to King Edward VII of England. This was done by the Transvaal government and the stone, cut then into nine large stones, was used to embellish the British crown jewels. Set in the crown and scepter of England, the diamonds posed no threat to diamond prices. In like manner, the fortune which had descended on Grand Fenwick, once turned over to the Duchess, could no longer hurt the economy of the country—though whether that condition would continue for the nine years which had to elapse before the chewing gum factory could be closed down and its unwanted profits ended was debatable.

In any case, having had her little lesson on stocks from the Count of Mountjoy, and having learned from him to her complete surprise that there were very many stock exchanges in the United States other than the famed New York Stock Exchange, the Duchess felt her confidence in her ability to get rid of the money restored. Accordingly she wrote to Mr. Balche and asked him to send her the names of all the stock markets in the United States of America and a list of all the stocks traded on those markets. She was sure that heavy investment in the shares of companies so small that they weren't even listed on the New York Stock Exchange would quickly put an end to her money problems.

Before sealing her letter, Gloriana had a brilliant idea. She loved gardening and each autumn and winter carefully budgeted what could be spent on new seed and bulbs in the coming spring. She was aware that some of the world's loveliest roses were developed in America, where they were patented. Also some entrancing iris and fuchsia in varieties beyond dreaming. To all these flowers she was devoted. Her garden budget each year had to be carefully laid out in purchases of new seed and of new plants.

But now, she recollected, no such care was needed. She could have acres of new American roses in all their intriguing varieties around the castle. And she could have other acres of iris and lovely cool drooping forests of flowering fuchsia. For a second she wondered whether it would be dishonest to spend some of the money on her personal pleasure in this way. But then she reflected that she had been given the job of disposing of the money without any stipulation as to method. And furthermore, the people of Grand Fenwick would enjoy the roses in the castle gardens quite as much as herself.

And so, at the bottom of the letter asking for the listing of stock exchanges, Gloriana added a postscript asking for seed, rose and other flower catalogues. And then she added another postscript saying that she didn't want to interfere in the slightest with the management of the Westwood Coal and Carriage Company.

"I expect the company will continue to lose money as it has in the past," she concluded. "I am really not interested in it at all, so if you can find a buyer at any price for the stocks I hold, please sell them."

CHAPTER XII

Light-years away from Grand Fenwick, in his business suite in Los Angeles, Ted Holleck surveyed the pattern of traffic eighteen floors below, threading its way along Sunset Boulevard. His profession was officially that of a stockbroker, and such he was, but in the new mode of that profession—a mode which would have enchanted the original brokers who first hawked shares in the Muscovy Company and the Hudson's Bay Company, more properly called "The Governor and Company of Adventurers of England Trading into Hudson's Bay." For Ted Holleck was an adventurer, as had been the early Americans before the nation had decided (surprisingly for so venturesome a people) that respectability, security and predictability are the hallmarks of worth.

Ted Holleck wore his hair as long as Daniel Boone and had dark curly sideburns coming to the corners of his mouth. His eyebrows were bushy and he brushed them every morning to be sure they stayed that way. His face had the craggy look once associated with the sculptures of Sir Eric Hill and now cultivated by folk guitarists. He was dressed in a black turtleneck sweater over which he wore a grass-green corduroy single-button jacket, without lapels. His trousers were black also and fitted as tight as leotards except about the ankles where a certain looseness was permitted. There were straps around the ends of his trousers which fitted under the instep of his shoes. His shoes were cowboy boots. He was handsome, strong, unmarried, just turned thirty, and there were throughout the United States several thousands of people who, when they prayed at all, prayed for his early death—preferably in a debtor's prison as soon as that institution could be revived.

Ted Holleck had, in fact, bought more companies out from underneath boards of directors than he had spent years on earth. He was, in the view of many, a wolf among the fat cattle of finance. He was a blackguard, a scoundrel, an unprincipled Cro-Magnon with a heart like that of a king cobra. But this was the view only of those who had been his victims. There were others who had enormously benefited from his activities, shareholders whose flagging companies had suddenly been thrust into unbounded riches; directors of obscure concerns manufacturing outdated water pumps, automobile parts, or gate hinges who had, as the result of the activities of Ted Holleck, become captains of industry, their holdings immensely increased and (a crowning glory) their names mentioned in the astringent little paragraphs printed in the business section of Time magazine.

Holleck had studied business law not at Harvard, where it is taught in the Wall Street or Back East fashion, but at UCLA where the same law takes on some of the excitement of Hollywood. And indeed he was a living proof that the surroundings in which a subject is taught are at least as important, if not more so, than the substance of the teaching itself. For, viewing, in his school days, the swirling opulence of West Los Angeles, the vigorous, childlike delight in whatever is new and daring and costs lots of money which is the atmosphere of West Los Angeles, Ted Holleck had absorbed much of this into his own spirit.

His law training was imbued with sparkling sunshine, movie affluence, surfboards and real estate development, and he early discovered that secret creed of all truly great lawyers, "The law is only the law when you get it into court. And then it is a matter of manipulating the jury." Except in federal cases. In federal cases, if guilty, the only real defense was to work for a mistrial and that could be relied upon to succeed at least 30 percent of the time. Odds of three to one against never quailed Ted Holleck.

This was the man who, surveying the swirl of fast traffic on Sunset Boulevard—the hippies and their successors, the producers, the actors, the agents, the real estate developers, and the construction tycoons, the clerks and the waiters and the cooks, and the television hopefuls; the whole mass whose job on earth it was to entertain, house, clothe, or feed their fellows at the highest rate procurable—meditated on the tax problem of Sunrise Space Enterprises, whose profits had fallen to a miserable thirty-five million dollars in the first quarter of the year. The prospects for the second quarter were poor for the reason that the company had neglected to undertake a serious market-research program in the past eighteen months. One was under way now, but its results could not be applied until the following year and so would not be reflected in current earnings.

He knew what Sunrise Space Enterprises had to do. It had to fire half of its top management because any management complex which could clear only thirty-five million dollars in the best quarter of the year, with the resources of Sunrise Space at its disposal, just wasn't doing its job. But rumors of management being fired would have an effect on shares and would bring thousands of wrathful shareholders around Ted Holleck's ears, so the cleanup there would have to be done quietly.

Meanwhile he decided he had better find a turkey somewhere for Sunset Space to merge with. If he could find a turkey which hadn't made a profit in years, in fact had been running at a loss for years, and which therefore was entitled to a vast tax write-off, and if he could merge with that turkey, then he could take advantage of the tax write-off for Sunset Space and that would be the equivalent of an increase in profits.

He glanced about his office, every item of which, he was glad to know, was tax deductible, including four pictures by Rouault which he personally abhorred and which were uninsured in the hope that they would be stolen, when he could deduct their greatly increased market value on his federal return as an uninsured loss.

It was not difficult to think of a candidate for absorption by Sunset Space. Holleck, like most in his profession, could reel off without hesitating a list of twenty companies whose earnings were negligible and who, under one provision of the law or other, were entitled to vast tax benefits. Oil companies, he was well aware, were particularly favored here, and among them he favored Rimrock Oil, which had managed to drill thirty-five dry holes before it got one in production—a feat which earned for Rimrock the respect and the sympathy of other oil operators most of whom reckoned to drill, on an average, five dry holes to one producer.

Rimrock, it was figured, could now bring in a further six producing wells without having to pay a penny of tax to the government, so concerned were the authorities over sustaining United States domestic oil production. The trouble about Rimrock, however, was that there were already three oil companies in the Sunrise Space conglomerate and the Antitrust Department just might block a further acquisition in that field as tending to monopoly.

Also in the Sunrise Space complex were several sulphur mining companies, four lead mines, two toy manufacturers, a drug company, cotton mill, refrigeration corporation, motion-picture producing company, motion-picture distributing company, a chain of movie houses, a publishing company, a chain of third-class newspapers, a pulp mill, shipping company, airlines and two night clubs—one in Los Angeles and the other in Boston. The capitalization of these companies was in the neighborhood of ten billion dollars and, the profits on this enormous capital investment being down to a few millions, they needed, as stated, a tax write-off.

Ted Holleck knew that the Sunrise tax experts had been over

every aspect of operations to see that the fullest advantage had been taken of all permissible deductions. The ball had been passed to him and he had to come up with a tax write-off of ten million dollars.

Unlike Gloriana, Holleck did not use a pin when seeking guidance on the stock market. He used a computer. He was one of the pioneers of computerized stock predictions, having devised a set of coordinates concerning companies which, when fed into his computer, resulted in a prediction concerning future earnings or future losses. The computer had so far proved comfortingly accurate. He flicked the button on the intercom on his desk and said, "Tell Jim to feed the coordinates on all the turkeys into the Think Tank. That would be Rimrock, Zigler Glass and Resin; Twenty Foresters; Isinglass Screens ... he knows the list. Oh, and don't forget Westwood Coal. Yes, I know there was that stock flurry and the shares have trebled in value. But I still think it's just some smart promoter who had better get out while he can. What I want is a rating showing the worst performers, say, over the past ten years. How long will that take? Tomorrow afternoon? Hell, I need it in a couple of hours. We are talking about money here, man, money. Ten million United States dollars and tomorrow won't do."

He snapped off the intercom and picked up a copy of *Blount's Financial Intelligencer*. It was a weekly magazine and this copy was two weeks old, but someone had brought it to him and said he should read some article in it. He leafed through the magazine and found a squib marked in red pencil at the bottom of one of the pages toward the end. It read:

Golden Gum

Overlooked in the recent surge in prices on the New York market has been Bickster and Company, operated at a loss for several years but now showing handsome profits with even greater earnings expected. The company manufactures a chewing gum with a wine flavor and the principal single shareholder is the Duchy of Grand Fenwick. Common shares are quoted at around 8 ¼, up five points from last year. Increased sales are laid to the anti-smoking campaign coupled with national advertising, particularly on television.

Bickster and Company, he reflected. That would be a nice little plum to steal. It could be added to the Sunrise Space network, or he might pull off a deal for Hastings Enterprises, or maybe he could do a little something for himself—broker's fees were fine and fat, but there were times when Ted Holleck wished he could get some of the action for himself. A few more words spoken into the intercom set his staff assembling all the pertinent facts concerning Bickster and Company. By the time he had returned from lunch at the table permanently reserved for him at Scandia's on the Strip, the full details of Bickster and Company were on his desk together with the information that the Think Tank believed that of the companies surveyed, Westwood Coal was the most likely to continue losing money.

Holleck considered these two pieces of information with care. This was the critical moment when, like a pirate captain in sight of a fast merchantman, he had to decide whether to attack immediately, bearing in mind the condition of the wind and set of the tide, or wait for a slight change of weather. Also if he were going to attack he must decide which of many possible plans to employ.

He could arrange a merger between Bickster and Westwood Coal which would be of enormous tax benefit to the former. He could propose to Hastings Enterprises to buy a majority of shares in the gum company to raid its profits and get Westwood Coal for Sunset Space as a tax write-off. The data before him indicated that Bickster was in the healthiest of financial conditions. There were no bank loans and no mortgages on equipment. It would not be difficult, just in the prospect of buying the company, to raise sufficient money as a loan to put the deal through, the loan to be secured by shares of stock when the deal was made. No deal, no loan and nobody hurt. He could in fact buy into Bickster himself.

The best plan of all, of course, would be to get a majority of the shares in Westwood Coal and a majority of those of Bickster. Then he could force a merger, as a major shareholder, of the two companies which would make him an immediate profit of several millions when the losses of Westwood Coal were written off against the profits of Bickster and Company.

He looked over the balance sheets of both companies, the comforting statements issued annually to stockholders, and taking out a solid gold propelling pencil with a small Cross of Amenhotep on top of it—it matched a larger cross which hung around his neck on a gold chain—he started scribbling on a block of eggshell-blue paper sparkling with golden glints.

The tax laws, as applied to corporations, he knew very thoroughly indeed. Twenty minutes of serious and uninterrupted work, using an elaborate abacus from twelfth-century China for calculating, produced a most gratifying result. Fifty-one percent of the shares of Westwood Coal could be had for just over three million dollars. Fifty-one percent of the shares of Bickster and Company could be had for perhaps twelve million dollars if he manipulated the bidding rightly—and he was an expert here. A total expenditure then of fifteen millions would make him—or any little syndicate he got together—the majority shareholder of both companies, when a merger could be put through. The merger, involving no more expenditure but merely an exchange of stock, would bring a tax rebate to the combined company of seventeen million dollars—that being the tax credit which had accrued over the gloomy decades of loss to Westwood Coal. This, of course, would not be refunded by the government but would be a credit handsomely reducing the taxes on the profits of Bickster and Company.

Elated, Ted Holleck grabbed a multicolored tam-o'-shanter from an old-fashioned hatrack which stood incongruously in one corner of his office and, entering the elevator, was lowered in this plexiglass cage to the slightly feminine foyer of the office building. He went out into the glittering street, turned left past the sumptuous doors of the Hoddaku Bank and Trust Company and into the discreet and over-English bar of the Golden Lion. The bar was, in fact, the Los Angeles equivalent of Hans's Bar on Wall Street in New York, though physically there was no resemblance. Standing at the bar was not allowed, perhaps because of the size of the martinis served which were gigantic. Customers sat at dark fumed-oak tables in booths upholstered in scarlet leather.

There were framed hunting scenes vaguely reminiscent of Cruikshank around the wall. The floor was of black-and-white imitation marble squares and covered with a mixture which looked like sawdust but was actually plastic. There were spittoons here and there, it being the conviction of the management that while the English had not yet learned not to spit in public they had learned not to spit on the floor. Over the bar was a stuffed fox head, the expression of the creature being one of fixed surprise. At Hans's Bar in New York, certain positions along the bar were by custom granted to particular members of brokerage companies. At the Golden Lion certain booths were also by custom allocated to particular clients, though the patronage was not made up exclusively of stockbrokers. It was as polyglot as the city, the only requirement being wealth. But a particular booth belonged to Ted Holleck and in this he sat while Charlie, a Mexican, dressed to have a raffish resemblance to an English stable hand, approached his table.

"Glass of acid?" asked Charlie.

"Right," said Holleck.

"How much money you made today, senor?" asked Charlie when he brought the martini. The management of the Golden Lion encouraged this kind of brashness between the help and its clients.

"Oh, I don't know," said Holleck. "Maybe two million. Maybe more."

"Two million," echoed Charlie. "In one day, senor?"

"I was tired," said Holleck. He was aware that several heads had turned in his direction.

"Wow," said Charlie. "They didn't clear that in a month with *Gone With the Wind*."

"Movies are for little boys," said Holleck. "The big money is out where the men play. Steel, plastics, rails—chewing gum. No romance, but lots of fun."

"Chewing gum?" said Charlie.

"Right," said Holleck, and Charlie knew from the shortness of that reply that the conversation was over. He went back to his post close to the service bar to mull over the exchange with Holleck. The most up-and-coming mod-type stockbroker on the West Coast, the real swinger, was interested in chewing gum. Of course Holleck had also mentioned steel, plastics and rails, but these were quite ordinary commodities for a stockbroker to touch on. No, Ted Holleck was interested in chewing gum and that information should be of interest to a certain party who sent him a ten-dollar bill occasionally for gossip passed on. So that night Charlie, at the Golden Lion in Los Angeles, wrote to Jimmy at Hans's Bar in New York saying, 'Hottest rumor around town right now is that Ted Holleck is interested in chewing gum. You know him—he's the real swinger. Next time you see a twenty-dollar bill, send me the half of it. Always your friend.

Charlie."

When Jimmie got the letter he passed the information on to Hans, who invested a judicious amount in the common stock of gum manufacturing companies. When four days later the price of shares of Bickster and Company, which had been edging up for some time, gained two points on a rumor that a Los Angeles syndicate was buying into the company, Hans sold his shares, collected his profits and gave a twenty-dollar bill to Jimmy.

Jimmy dutifully sent ten dollars to his colleague at the Golden Lion with a brief note saying the weather in New York was cold for the time of year.

Charlie puzzled over this for a while and then mentioned to one or two of his customers that New York was getting excited about the boom in ski equipment. It was the most he could make of it.

CHAPTER XIII

Holleck, for whom the raiding of companies had become an art of which he was the master, had no difficulty in securing a majority of the shares of both Bickster and Company and Westwood Coal. It was said of him, and with some truth, that he could steel the sheet from underneath a sleeping man without the sleeper ever being aware of it. A few telephone calls and telegrams, a rumor adroitly planted here and there—his visit to the Golden Lion had been no mere expression of exuberance at the prospect of a multi-million-dollar gain—a mention in the financial columns of *Newsweek*, a photograph of himself in *Playboy* about to pop a stick of chewing gum into his mouth and an insistent denial to all his friends that he was himself acquiring shares in anything—these were but a portion of the forces he organized for the raid on the two companies, which he did not regard as very difficult in any case.

Holleck did not like the business of getting lists of stockholders, canvassing among them, propagandizing them into voting for mergers or throwing out an entrenched management when obtaining his aims. All this was bludgeon work which did not appeal to his nature. In an age of mass and saturation communication, he used mass and saturation communication to spread rumors, true and false, which influenced spending and money flow. He bought shares in tens or in blocks of thousands. Sometimes he staged an obvious raid on one company to divert attention from the fact that he was in fact raiding another. Though he had never studied the military arts he knew by instinct the cardinal rules of fighting, principal among them the injunction to hit hard, fast and where least expected—which was sometimes at the strongest point.

He had no trouble whatever in getting control of Westwood Coal. Mr. Balche had been instructed by Gloriana to sell. He put the shares on the market and Holleck's syndicate grabbed up 51 percent in one swoop at five and a half, which sent them soaring up to seven for a day when they steadied at six and a quarter as a result of the magic associated with Holleck's reputation.

Bickster and Company was not so easy but provided no great difficulties. The shares were high priced though not overpriced, and they went up—as Holleck had intended—following the rumors he deliberately sowed. They went up, in fact, first two points and then gained a further two and a half, and at this point Holleck sent an anonymous donation of $50,000 to a research center in Rio de Janeiro to investigate the relationship between skin cancer among North Americans and the national habit of chewing gum. Mention of this line of research and of the large sum privately donated to its investigation soon appeared in the newspapers of Brazil, was transmitted to the newspapers in the United States, and produced a fall in chewing gum sales and a sharper fall in the price of shares.

Having just boosted the shares and then started them on the road downhill, Holleck reaped a harvest from the profit-taking, buying up all the shares offered by those who had decided not to risk a further decline in their price. It is a principle of the stock exchanges of the world that once a run starts on a stock it is hard to stop without big money and the passage of time. People sell and then justify the sale by repeating the reasons for which they sold, thus encouraging others to sell. So Holleck acquired the needed shares in the company, stopping when he and the members of his syndicate had control.

It was easy then to force a merger between the two companies, thereafter gaining a huge tax credit for Bickster. As soon as the news reached the market, the shares of both companies soared. An automatic increase in the profits of Bickster was guaranteed by the tax relief, and the shares of what was now Bickster Chicle and Coal doubled in value on the following day.

By the end of the month they had gone up to 150 percent of their previous values. This was plainly the time for a stock split to cash in on the vast public confidence in Bickster Chicle and Coal.

A two-for-one split brought the value of the shares down to twenty-five dollars, but so avidly was the new issue bought up that the new shares were soon being offered at forty dollars and readily commanding that price. The bewildered Mr. Balche found that in the two months which had lapsed between his instructions from Gloriana to sell the shares in Westwood Coal and the merger of Westwood Coal with Bickster and Company, Grand Fenwick's holdings were now worth forty million dollars.

"That's a remarkable woman," exclaimed Balche, watering his geraniums. "How I should like to meet her. Starting with a six-million-dollar investment in a completely worthless company, she has converted her capital into forty million dollars plus a vast share of the enormously increased profits of Bickster Chicle and Coal. She's the tigress of Wall Street. What cool courage. What disdainful control of the whole situation. And what a remarkable combination—Gloriana the Twelfth of Grand Fenwick and Ted Holleck of Los Angeles. Joan of Arc allied with the Beatles. Upon my word, I have lived to see strange times."

Mr. Balche, of course, never for a moment doubted that Gloriana was working very closely and secretly with Ted Holleck and never for a moment suspected that neither had heard of the other. He felt at first a little betrayed, a little left out. After all, he was the Duchy's financial agent in the United States. He might at least, he felt, have been given a hint of this vast and daring financial campaign against Wall Street which was now being launched from parts as diverse as Grand Fenwick and Los Angeles. And yet he knew enough of human nature to admit that any sharing of the secret would be eminently dangerous. He consoled himself with the thought that he could claim, when the whole thing was uncovered, to have played a not so insignificant part. Was he not, after all, the neutral ground on which these two mighty warriors of finance, Gloriana XII and Ted Holleck, met? Wasn't it to him that Gloriana came when she wished to buy or sell shares? And wasn't it to him also that Ted Holleck had come when he was seeking shares in Bickster and Company? Yes, indeed. Picking a few dead leaves from among his geraniums, and eying with satisfaction the new growth of fat buds which promised a profusion of flowers in the weeks ahead, he had to admit that he was the essential catalyst which permitted these two dynamic forces to work together ... to interact with such dramatic effect.

Raised in a tradition of discretion and of confidence, Mr. Balche would never dream of mentioning the name of Gloriana to Ted Holleck or the name of Ted Holleck to Gloriana. Whatever their direct correspondence might be with each other (and he was sure there must be much of it), it was plain that when they dealt through him, they wanted their connection kept completely secret. To refer to it at all then would be a blunder on his part of monstrous proportions.

He, Joseph Balche, was the cover for this brilliant combination—the guardian of a secret which he was sure would one day (and that day quite soon) shake the whole financial world to its deepest foundations.

In his correspondence with Gloriana, Mr. Balche was now in something of a quandary as to what attitude to adopt. Surely it would be now entirely gauche and naive to write telling her that her original investment was now worth forty million dollars when he was quite sure that she had made that investment with a cool head and the clearest financial foresight and planning. On the other hand, should he continue to sell stock in the new company? He decided he should not. His last instruction from Her Grace had concerned the selling of stock in the old company, Westwood Coal. That had achieved its end. He had now only to wait further instructions and in the meantime cooperate fully with Ted Holleck in any plans that gentleman (certainly Gloriana's partner) had to make.

That Ted Holleck was Gloriana's partner seemed quite confirmed by the curious fact that Holleck had bought only enough shares to give him a firm majority control of Bickster and Company and Westwood Coal—the rest of them remaining in the hands of the Duchess.

When then Mr. Balche received a letter from Gloriana telling him that he was to spend the money realized from the sale of the Westwood Coal shares in the purchase of Rimrock Oil, he assumed that another daring financial raid was being planned. He bought the shares as instructed. They were worth four and an eighth and were declining with the news that Rimrock had obtained an oil concession in Portugal, drilled four wells and got only salt water for its pains.

Ten million dollars were expended on buying up the shares of Rimrock either from dealers or on the open market, and this money did not exhaust what was available to Gloriana from sale of previous holdings plus the four million dollars' cash gain she had made in acquiring Westwood Coal. The shares were acquired and Mr. Balche waited. Nothing happened. A week went by and then two weeks. By the end of the month, another dry hole having come in, the Rimrock

Oil shares were down to two and a half and Mr. Balche decided to write to Gloriana and tell her she had lost about four million on the deal. He had the letter written and was on the point of mailing it when the long anticipated telephone call arrived.

"Holleck here," said the caller. "I want Rimrock and am directed to you. What are you asking?"

"I have no instructions from my client to sell," said Balche. "Do you wish to make an offer?"

"Yes," said Holleck. "A half above the market, whatever it might be."

"I will contact my client and let you know," said Mr. Balche. "It will take at least two weeks."

There was a silence and Holleck said, "I can wait. Call me when to send the money."

Such confidence that the deal was to be consummated made Mr. Balche smile for it quite confirmed his theory that Holleck and Gloriana were partners. When a letter arrived from Gloriana two weeks later telling him to sell the stock to whoever wanted it, Mr. Balche called Holleck and said he could have all the stock at half a point above the market, which would be one and three quarters.

"Thanks," said Holleck. "I'm buying fifty-one percent of the shares. No more. I'll send my check."

The check, when it arrived, was signed by the treasurer of Sunrise Space. Within a month Sunrise Space announced a merger between Rimrock Oil and Indian Head Petroleum, one of its subsidiaries, with three shares of Rimrock Oil equated at one share of

Indian Head. The value of the new shares dipped and suddenly soared with the drilling of a producing well in Portugal. A stock split was announced and a further fifteen million dollars in shares accrued to the account of Gloriana and the Duchy of Grand Fenwick. The total holdings of the young Duchess were now in the neighborhood of fifty-five million dollars.

Things began at this point to happen at a speed which made Mr. Balche dizzy and left him quite confused, for he was made aware only of the results without knowing of the details which led to them. As closely as he could follow what was going on, Bickster Chicle and Coal merged with Monolith Productions (motion pictures) and John and Mary Publishing (school texts)—the diversity was to escape a charge by the Antitrust Department of monopoly—and the three merged companies then took over Western Bank and Trust. What all this was about Mr. Balche could not divine at the time for no immediate profit or increase in share values was apparent from these mergers.

However, the pattern became a little clearer when Western Bank and Trust was swallowed; for it came out that the bank had lent beyond its strength and held mortgages and other enforceable paper in a transit company, two gold mines, a shipping line, an airline, five massive real-estate developments, and a steel plant. These companies were forced into bankruptcy and their assets seized by the principal creditor—now Bickster Pinot Chicle and Coal Monolith Productions and John and Mary. And out of the whole financial whirlwind emerged, when the dust had settled, a massive complex of companies called Pinot Productions, itself a rival to Sunset Space and the master of a conglomerate ranging from school texts to blast furnaces. Shares in Pinot Productions were worth on the market eighty-five dollars, and behind this financial juggernaut which loomed now over Wall Street and the stock exchanges of the nation was beginning to emerge a young, attractive and mysterious figure whose name was mentioned with awe in financial circles—the Duchess Gloriana XII of Grand Fenwick.

CHAPTER XIV

The first million, it is well known, is the hardest to make. Thereafter the second is easier, the third easier still and so on. In Grand Fenwick's case the first several millions had been donated to the Duchy without any effort on their part. And from then on, no matter what efforts the Duchess Gloriana made to get rid of it, the money continued to pile up in Himalayan proportions. Without planning it in the least, she made the Duchy a major shareholder in the multi-million-dollar Pinot Productions Corporation, and a shareholder of vast power in the equally huge Sunrise Space Enterprises. Her share of the profits from these holdings amounted to further millions of dollars each quarter, and all the time the price of shares held continued to rise so that even Mr. Balche could not tell at any one moment just what was the value of the holdings of the Duchy of Grand Fenwick in American stocks.

Gloriana was herself quite unaware of the gargantuan fortune which she was amassing by mischance. Her only source of financial information was the *London Times*, which arrived irregularly depending upon the view Salat, the French bus driver, took of world affairs and the glory of France.

The single copy of the *Times* which was delivered to Grand Fenwick traveled an established route throughout the castle. It went first to the Prime Minister, now David Bentner, leader of the Labor or Dilutionist party, who turned immediately to the sports pages for he was an avid supporter of the Tottenham Hotspurs Football Club in England. (In summer he had to be content with cricket scores and favored Hampshire, though cricket is not, by its nature, a competitive game.) Mountjoy usually sent his man down to Bentner's office to get the paper about midday so that he could glance at the Court Circular and what he called the "foreign intelligence." He also read the leader articles, liked to speculate at the behest of what cabinet minister in England a particular point had been made, and occasionally wrote to the editor correcting the English used in an article. He had managed to carry on a correspondence of some months with readers of the *Times* on the difference between the words "special" and "especial" and vigorously denounced the American habit of turning any noun into an adverb by the addition of the suffix "wise."

After Mountjoy, Gloriana usually managed to get the *Times* and these days turned immediately to the stock listings. The only stocks she had been interested in were Westwood Coal and Rimrock Oil. Shortly after she had instructed Mr. Balche to buy these they had both disappeared from *The New York Times* listings, and Gloriana assumed that the companies had gone into bankruptcy and were no longer in existence. Since this was exactly what she wanted she was quite happy about the matter, and although she wasn't quite clear about the figure, she believed that she had managed at last to get rid of all the money except perhaps for a few thousand dollars which might remain after bankruptcy proceedings out of the millions invested.

She was, however, a little disturbed one day, in going through the stock lists, to come upon the name "Pinot Productions" with after it a quotation of 135 ½ per share. She asked Mountjoy about that. "Someone over there is taking our name," she said. "Look at that." And she showed him the listing.

"Nothing for us to be concerned about, Your Grace," Mountjoy replied. "Pinot, after all, is the name of a wine available in several parts of France. The Pinot blanc of the Graves district is almost respectable. There is really nothing to stop an American corporation putting the word Pinot in its name."

"I wonder what Pinot Productions produces?" said Gloriana.

"Money," said Mountjoy. "It is the object of all commercial activity."

"Tell me, Bobo," said Gloriana, "when the name of a stock no longer appears in these lists, does that mean that the company concerned went broke?"

"Not necessarily," said Mountjoy. "It may have merged. It may have changed its name. There are other explanations. But it is a suspicious sign when it ceases to be listed."

With that Gloriana was content. She had received no letters

from Balche for some weeks. She assumed that she soon would get a letter saying that her investment funds were exhausted and she noted that there was no longer a listing of Bickster and Company on the financial pages of the *Times*. So perhaps that had gone broke, too, and thus the financial difficulties of the Duchy would be at an end.

When the patent roses and bulbs and flower seeds which she had ordered through Balche arrived she was glad that enough of the money had been saved to provide these for the castle gardens. And she was glad, too, when a small heavy crate arrived on Salat's bus, containing the special piece of equipment which Dr. Kokintz had required. The crate was labeled "Carriage Fully Paid" so there wasn't even an airplane freight bill to worry about.

Kokintz was delighted to receive the apparatus. It was taken immediately to his laboratory and he had four men working for a week installing it in a section which he had cleared near one of the walls. Gloriana went to see the apparatus when it was in place and was disappointed to find nothing more than two highly polished metal lenses with four red squares painted on them. They were set up to face each other only an inch or two apart, and in the center of them was a tuning fork. (She hated tuning forks because in her father's day she had had to take singing lessons, and her teacher was constantly producing a tuning fork, striking it, and demanding that she sing the note, which she couldn't.)

"What is it for?" she asked.

"Your Grace," said Kokintz, "if I tell you you won't understand. Better I get some results. Then I will show you the results and everything will be clear."

"Well, is it something to do with heat, light, or sound?" asked Gloriana, who remembered that much from her physics teaching.

"Heat, light and sound," said Kokintz, smiling. "Once they were nice and separate. Now they are all aspects of the same thing. Well, of the three of them, it has most to do with sound."

With that Gloriana had to be content. But she turned to the planting of the new roses and bulbs and flower seeds in the castle gardens and began to think of a vast garden party when everybody could come and see the enchanting floral display in the castle grounds.

When the bombshell burst, the advance warning was so subtle that Gloriana did not get the signal. She received one day a letter from England—from the *London Times*. She thought it might be a bill for the renewal of the Duchy's subscription, but the bills usually came in stone-colored envelopes and this was a chaste white envelope with the *Times* letterhead discreetly engraved on one corner. Also it was addressed personally to her, and the typing of the address was almost as beautiful as the letterhead. She opened it with an expectation of pleasure and found inside a short letter from the Financial Editor of the newspaper begging the favor of an interview with her on her activities in the American stock market.

"Your Grace is perhaps not unaware," the letter said, "of the universal admiration which your calculation and daring have aroused in financial circles not only in the United States but on the London exchange as well. That Your Grace has entered the world of finance is now no longer a secret and we would be very happy if you could see your way now to discussing your investment theories and perhaps give your views of the long-range future of conglomerates and the growing involvement of the small speculator in mutual funds."

The letter surprised Gloriana. She turned to the envelope to see whether it was indeed addressed to her. She had no idea what a conglomerate was. It sounded like something that Kokintz might know of—a collection of jelly-like substances perhaps resembling frog's eggs. And mutual funds? There was a Mutual Insurance Company somewhere, she believed, but she had no connection with it. Surely there was some mistake.

She kept the letter for three days without replying, Mountjoy's training that delay was always an advantage asserting itself here. Then she decided that she had better let someone else in on her secret—the method she had devised of getting rid of the unneeded money by investing it in the stock market.

So she told her husband Tully about it over breakfast, and he choked on his buttered toast but otherwise suffered no harm when she assured him that she had got rid of almost everything in under seven months. Then a little nervous, she told Mountjoy, visiting his office herself instead of summoning him, which was quite unusual. But she knew that if she went to him he would be less angry if she had, in fact, done anything wrong. She wasn't quite sure of the propriety of even titular heads of state investing in American stocks. Mountjoy was aghast. His face went quite white. He was for a moment—but only for a moment—without a single phrase, without indeed a word, to utter to express his feelings.

"...so I got rid of it all," Gloriana concluded hurriedly, "and now there's this funny letter from the *London Times*. What do you think I ought to do about it?"

Mountjoy ignored the letter. "Your Grace," he exclaimed, "you overwhelm me. You leave me in silent and stricken admiration. Never in all my experience or all my reading have I heard of anything so completely magnificent."

"Oh, I'm glad I didn't do anything wrong," murmured Gloriana, blushing prettily.

"Wrong?" cried Mountjoy. "What you did was so absolutely right it would bring cheers—loud cheers—for you from the wizards of finance of every nationality. The Rothschilds would be on their knees before you. John Maynard Keynes would regard as wasted every moment he did not spend in your presence.

"Your Grace, yours was a stroke which bears the clear hallmark of genius. Utter simplicity. How to get rid of money without disrupting anyone's economy? Of course, invest it in the stock market in the purchase of the very worst stocks that can be found. For money is at base only an expression of public confidence. And if you can transform money into something in which the public has no confidence, then the money disappears. And nobody is hurt in the slightest. I am humbled, my lady. This is the classic solution which I should long ago have been able to present to you. Instead you have shown it to me."

"Will you tell Mr. Bentner for me then?" asked Gloriana. "I

think you could explain it to him better than I can."

"I will be delighted," said Mountjoy.

"And about this letter? Why do you suppose they would want an interview with me?"

"Your Grace, you have demonstrated such a genius in financial affairs that I am sure this is just the first of many letters which you will receive. Reflect for a moment that the stock market has always been used to make money and this is probably the first time in history that it has ever been used to lose money deliberately. You have stumbled on a device for curbing inflation which may have enormous value for government everywhere. No longer will it be necessary to siphon off surplus money by taxation, leaving the government a harvest of popular ill will and also the problem of what to do with the taxes thus accumulated. You have found a method of making surplus and inflationary money disappear.

"Of course you must give your interview to the *Times*. Keynes's theories concerning deficit financing will utterly pale compared with your discovery of deflationary speculation."

"Well, what are conglomerates? They want to ask me about them," persisted Gloriana.

Mountjoy picked up the letter and read it through. "Do not fear, Your Grace," he said. "I will instruct you on all these terms and, if you wish, be present during the course of the interview. As for conglomerates, the whole theory concerning them is embraced in the ancient country saying, 'Do not put all your eggs in one basket.' It is merely the application to Wall Street and the world of finance of a maxim that small farmers have known and used for years. In short, you are safer if everything you own is not in one crop."

And so Gloriana, ignorant of the fact that her name had become one of awe and admiration in the world of finance, and that articles concerning her wizardry were always appearing in *Baron's Weekly*, *Fortune* and other widely read publications, wrote to the financial editor of the *Times* of London and the interview was arranged.

CHAPTER XV

Mr. Jack Sweeting, financial editor of the *Times* of London, was quite swept off his feet by Gloriana. An Englishman, he had, by nature, an attitude of protective gallantry toward women provided they did not (as, alas, so often happened in the modern world) desert their femininity and demonstrate learning and intelligence. Of such women he was nervous, if not afraid, and therefore his attitude toward them was one of cold politeness.

He had suspected that Gloriana XII of Grand Fenwick might be such a woman—a lamentable product, perhaps, of the London School of Economics (a drab institution which lent a wintry touch to the Thames embankment even in the height of summer), rather than of an Elizabeth Arden beauty spa.

He found her completely charming—lovely, gentle, witty and gracious. She made tea for him herself (Twining's Number 2 on the advice of Mountjoy, who was up on these things) and took him for a tour of the Duchy which, the spring now burgeoning, was not unlike a tour through Camelot.

Although an economist of world standing, Jack Sweeting was country bred and of the generation which could remember the English countryside between the wars. Grand Fenwick reminded him of that departed England. He met flocks of white-faced sheep, their fleeces heavy upon them, being taken to upland pastures where the grass was now freshening. He heard long-forgotten sounds, like the slow creak of farm carts rumbling down the road, the twittering of hedge sparrows and the piping of curlews. He heard also the silence of the countryside during which only the wind speaks, touching here and there the sere stalks of leftover grass and the twigs of hawthorn and elder, now misted with green. In fact, he was so overcome by Gloriana and her country that she could have produced answers which were completely nonsensical to his questions and he, completely bowled over, would gallantly have made of them, if not pearls of wisdom, at least beads of sense.

Actually Gloriana did very well with the interview. She said, under the schooling of Mountjoy, that she suspected that the United States would very soon legislate in the field of conglomerates to prevent the manipulation of industries for financial profit unrelated to their produce. (She had that sentence by heart and was very relieved not to be pressed on the subject.) She said that foreign investment would without a doubt be an increasingly powerful factor in all stock markets and that this represented a healthy growth of international capitalism, competing with international communism. She said that the adoption of a set of international values for currencies, which were not changeable, would greatly facilitate international trade and investment.

"If trade is international, then we must have an international kind of money," she said. "Wouldn't you like a fresh cup of tea, Mr. Sweeting? I am afraid yours is cold."

Mr. Sweeting accepted the tea and asked what monetary unit for international exchange and investment Gloriana had in mind. Mountjoy suggested the Swiss franc, in which there was widespread public confidence backed by the neutrality of Switzerland and the vast experience of its bankers. A few more questions in this area produced some rather muddy answers because Gloriana really didn't know anything about Swiss francs or Portuguese escudos (suggested by Sweeting). But she made the point that a housewife living in an international city would be very much handicapped in her marketing if she had to pay Chinese yen for her laundry, French francs for her clothing and English pounds for her meat.

"Is the European Common Market a step in the direction you are advocating?"

"Yes, it is," said Gloriana, who really didn't know anything about the European Common Market except that it was generally reckoned a good thing.

"Would Grand Fenwick be interested in joining the European Common Market?" asked Sweeting.

Gloriana glanced at Mountjoy. She really didn't know what to say to that.

"Grand Fenwick has no place in the European Common

Market," said Mountjoy. "Our two principal products, wine and wool, find their own market without competition. We do not need the cooperation and aid of other nations in selling them. Common markets arise from common causes. We have no common economic cause with others."

Sweeting now turned to Gloriana's own investment policy. He half hoped Mountjoy would go away so that he could question her closely here, but the Count was as firmly fixed by the side of Gloriana as the castle was around her, and so Sweeting had to go ahead with his questioning with Mountjoy standing by as guard.

"You have yourself demonstrated a remarkable knowledge of the New York stock market, following a bold investment policy which has roused widespread admiration," said Sweeting. "Can you, in a sentence or two, summarize your philosophy of investment?"

Gloriana had her reply down pat. "I think the very best attitude for anyone investing in the stock market is to make up his mind to lose money," said Gloriana. "I don't see how any other attitude could possibly work." Mr. Sweeting smiled. She was being cagey with him, reiterating advice which, he recalled, had once been given by Baron Rothschild.

"And you entered the market then with the prospect before you of losing your total investment?" he asked.

"Oh yes," said Gloriana. "That was never for one moment out of my mind. I just kept on investing and investing. And you know what happened."

"The world knows," said Mr. Sweeting. "One of the most

remarkable feats of the present century. I am sure that you undertook a great deal of study of the market, however, before starting your investment program."

"No," said Gloriana, "I can't say that I did. I had an objective in mind and I persisted until I achieved that objective. That is really all that I can say. I don't think that there is anything extraordinary in what I did."

"Your name has been linked, in connection with your raid on Wall Street, with the brilliant young American financier, Mr. Ted Holleck," said Sweeting. "Is it true that you were working in close cooperation with Mr. Holleck in making your choice of investments?"

"Mr. who?" said Gloriana.

"Holleck."

"I'm afraid I have never heard of him," said the Duchess. "I did all my ordering of stocks through Mr. Joseph Balche, who is the financial agent of Grand Fenwick in the United States. He sent me all my seeds too."

"Seeds?"

"Yes—seeds and bulbs. And the new roses which I showed you in the garden."

Sweeting, nonplused, repeated his question. "You are quite sure that you had not heard of Mr. Holleck?" he asked. "He followed almost precisely the same investment program as yourself."

"I really have never heard of him," said Gloriana. "And if he followed the same program as I did, then maybe he had the same method of selecting his stocks."

"Can you show me what that method is?" asked Sweeting, returning to this question.

For answer Gloriana, ignoring Mountjoy, secured the financial page of the *Times*, got a pin from the arm of the sofa on which she was sitting and stuck it, her eyes shut, into the page.

Sweeting laughed. "I shouldn't have asked the question," he said. "And I suppose your answer is as good as any."

That concluded the interview. Sweeting drove his rented car to Marseilles, where he caught a plane back to London and spent the evening mulling over his notes and working them up into an interview which he hoped would convey to his readers both the charm of the Duchess and her astute grasp of world finance.

He succeeded admirably. He had secured his interview on a Tuesday, and since haste is frowned upon at the *Times* (only gossip is urgent; news has a solid and lasting quality) his interview did not appear until the following Monday. The Monday *Times* did not reach Grand Fenwick until the succeeding Wednesday because Salat was annoyed that Great Britain had objected to Paris as the site for the peace talks between the United States and Northern Afghanistan. (Salat looked upon Grand Fenwick as an ally of Great Britain.) So a pleasant eight days elapsed during which Gloriana did her gardening before the bombshell broke.

The paper, of course, went first to Bentner as Prime Minister, who missed the story completely since it was in the financial section which he never read. He was concerned only with cricket and the body-line bowling controversy of some years previous, now being resurrected. It should then have gone to Mountjoy, but Bentner instead took it to Dr. Kokintz to show him a report on a French rocket being sent to the planet Jupiter. It would take three years to get there, and Kokintz said that that represented an act of faith not in physics but in the government of France which had been tottering for a twelvemonth.

Kokintz was busy with his curious apparatus of the two hemispheres with the tuning fork between them and laid the *Times* aside, and Mountjoy's secretary had to hunt the whole castle before he found it under a lump of some curious substance which Kokintz was using as a paperweight. He took it to Mountjoy, who, after glancing at the foreign news and sighing for the great days of Balkan politics, turned to the financial pages.

There he found the interview with the Duchess. There was a two-column picture of Her Grace in her full regalia and the interview ran below the picture and was of the extent of a full column and a half. Mountjoy began reading it with a sense of pleasure. How good it was, he reflected, to read a paper like the *Times*, which didn't indulge in superlatives or hysteria, but in elegant, almost classical English set forth the facts with balance and humor.

It wasn't until he got to the fourth paragraph that he received any kind of shock. The fourth paragraph contained a qualifying clause stating that the Duchess Gloriana XII had astonished the financial world by her massive raid on American stocks which had made her and the Duchy the most powerful single shareholder in the two American billion-dollar conglomerates—Sunrise Space and Pinot Productions. The holdings of the Duchy were reckoned to be in the neighborhood of seven hundred million dollars and increasing in value each day.

Stunned, Mountjoy read the whole thing over slowly and then reached with a trembling hand for the telephone. "Get me Mr. Jack Sweeting of the *London Times*," he said.

"I'm sorry," said the operator, "but we don't have any outside lines, as you know, Your Excellency."

Mountjoy replaced the telephone. He stared at the paper, which he had let fall from nerveless hands on the desk before him. Seven hundred million dollars. His brain seemed to become liquid. He passed his hands over his face as if to peel off with his fingers some enchantment which had intervened between himself and reality.

"Impossible," he said. "Impossible. *The Times* has blundered." But he knew that the *Times* never blundered, that the *Times* was always right and that by some witchcraft beyond his control and beyond the control of the Duchess or perhaps anybody in Grand Fenwick the Duchy had been made heir to a fortune which was the equivalent of the total national budget for seven thousand years.

"My God," he cried. "This is the curse of Croesus. Everything we touch turns to gold."

CHAPTER XVI

The news was too appalling to be accepted immediately by anyone. It had to be rejected, to be denounced, to be decried and disbelieved before it could be reduced to such a size that Gloriana, Bentner, Tully and Mountjoy could cope with it. Gloriana said it was a joke—a horrible, outrageous kind of joke at the expense of Grand Fenwick—and added that the Duchy ought to sue the *Times*. Bentner said it was an attempt by entrenched capitalists to somehow bolster a flagging stock market by solemnly insisting that those who had lost a fortune in stocks had actually gained a super fortune. Mountjoy spent hours combing through the back issues of the *Times*, and through the stock listings, until he came to the issue in which Westwood Coal and Carriage disappeared. He compared this date with the date of Gloriana's letters to Balche and announced firmly that some frightful error had been made by the *Times*; for plainly Westwood Coal and Carriage, in which Gloriana had put her money initially, had been sunk with all hands—a thoroughly bad metaphor which he permitted himself in his extreme agitation.

Only Tully Bascomb was prepared to face the truth and demand that, instead of developing theories of their own, the Duchy obtain from Balche a full analysis of its American holdings.

The matter was viewed as so grave that a cable was sent to Mr. Balche asking him for a full description of the holdings and their value. Bentner himself went into France to dispatch the cable, for this duty could not be entrusted to the temperamental Salat.

From the description which came in reply it was made unmistakably clear that Grand Fenwick held extensive interests in every branch of industrial activity in the United States from plumbing to planetary exploration. Stock splits were occurring at the rate of one a month in the companies in which the Duchy had shares, and with a rising market the split shares were soon selling for close to the value of the original shares. In short, Grand Fenwick's fortune was swelling like a loaf in a warm oven, and Mr. Balche was of the opinion that by the end of the year the Duchy might be the owner of close to a billion dollars' worth of American stocks of one sort or another.

This was the terrible news that now had to be put before the nation in an emergency session of the Council of Freemen. Gloriana was in tears. It was all her fault, she said. She had failed her people. Given the task of getting rid of the riches which threatened the economy and the way of life of the nation, she had instead enormously multiplied those riches so that they now mounted to a sum so vast that it practically could not be disposed of. Tully and

Mountjoy consoled her in some measure by insisting that she had done her best and the result had been entirely beyond her control and so was not her fault.

"Whether we like it or not, we are millionaires," was Bentner's comment. "Makes you sick to think that the wages paid to the workingmen of Grand Fenwick all added together for perhaps a century wouldn't amount to that stock market fortune got together without a tap of work in a matter of a few months."

"I was trying to get rid of it," said Gloriana between sobs.

"So you were, Ma'am," said Bentner. "But you hadn't a chance among those capitalist wolves on Wall Street." And he gave a look of greatest enmity to the Count of Mountjoy. Although this was a complete parody of the actual situation, since it was the Duchess who had played the wolf on Wall Street, Mountjoy was delighted at the hostile look he received from Bentner. This, he reflected, was the way things should be—Capital versus Labor. That made for sound government. When Capital and Labor began to embrace each other any nation, he knew, was doomed to fall.

"I think it should be the part of the government to take on itself the responsibility for this disaster," said Mountjoy vindictively, watching Bentner squirm. "The alternative would be to place the responsibility on the shoulders of Her Grace—no gentleman, no man, would ever contemplate such a thing." He was rather happy actually. If Bentner could be held entirely responsible, then there was a possibility of unseating him at the next general election, for the post of Leader of the Loyal Opposition did not entirely suit Mountjoy.

But Gloriana would not hear of such a plan.

"The task was given to me," she said. "I accepted it willingly and gladly. I failed and I myself must go before my people and tell them that it is I who am responsible."

And so she did, at the special session of the Council of Freemen. She outlined the whole story and her plans for getting rid of the money and she made a very good case for herself. She pointed out that it was common knowledge that huge sums of money were frequently lost on the stock market and they were more likely to be lost if the investor knew nothing of the market or of the stocks in which an investment was made.

To be sure that she knew nothing whatever of any of the stocks invested in, she had selected them by sticking a pin in the financial pages of the *Times* of London. Her choice had been a good one and she had managed to lose something like four million dollars in four weeks—a record of which she was proud. There was a little flutter of applause around the chamber at this point, although some of the upland farmers who at times had difficulty making ends meet looked a trifle apoplectic.

It seemed, however, Gloriana continued, that her choice had not been a good one. She had bought all the shares in a dying company for the Duchy and then discovered that the company had, in cash, a sum of ten million dollars, so that, trying her best to lose six millions, she had actually made a cash profit of four millions. (One of the uplanders fainted here and had to be carried out and revived.)

So Gloriana unfolded the whole tale, of which she now had details from Balche, and pointed out how her very best efforts to unload money were thwarted by the American financier Ted Holleck who, unknown to her, had bought a controlling interest in the companies in which Grand Fenwick had invested. His object, however, had been the opposite of that of the Duchess and, having a majority interest and vast power and experience, he had been able to turn to gold all that she had tried to turn to dross.

"I come before you as the sovereign of my people to confess my failure," said the Duchess bravely. "Despite my best endeavors I have amassed a fortune in stocks which I am told is valued now at close to one billion dollars, which would make millionaires of every family in the Duchy . ."

Whatever else the Duchess was going to say was swept aside as members leaped to their feet shouting, "Long live the Duchess Gloriana the Twelfth." But for the respect in which they held her position they would have carried her on their shoulders through the streets. It has never fallen to any nation in the history of man and finance that each family in that nation should become heir to a million dollars. All restraint was cast away—all memories of the misfortunes which had attended the disbursement of the original Gum Money were forgotten. A million dollars for every family in Grand Fenwick? There was not a member in the chamber, with the exception of Mountjoy, who was not at that moment contemplating a world tour in his own private yacht.

It was Mountjoy who brought them to their senses. Obtaining

the Speaker's eye (when that worthy had restored some semblance of order) and begging leave of the Duchess, he made it perfectly clear that there was no intention on his part as Leader of the Opposition that any portion of the money should enter the Duchy's economy. Bentner, as if stifling, made the same announcement, and the uplander fainted again. But Bentner had had a lesson in riches and he, taking over from Mountjoy, said that the government would have to be overthrown and a new party system, adhering to different principles, would have to be installed before the money would be divided among the people.

"And what will you have if this is done?" he asked. "Honest workingmen producing their sustenance from their labor and the land? Happy families, decently housed and living in peace and kindness with their neighbors? No, indeed. You will have a population gone hog-wild with wealth. Champagne in every bathtub and a new wife for any man who wants one. That's what you'll have."

At the mention of a new wife for every man who wanted one there was a rather vulgar cheer from the back benches, but the sense of what Bentner had to say began to go home. He was not a dramatic orator, but he spoke, when aroused, bluntly and in terms that his countrymen understood.

"You, Ted Williams," he said, pointing to a member opposite him, "how much money did you owe after the last government handout?"

"Seventy-five quid," said Williams, unabashed.

"And how much do you owe now?"

"None. I paid it all off."

"Yes, and with wages you earned yourself so that you are your own man," said Bentner. "You didn't pay with money that fell into your lap and left you looking around for more to fall from the same place. We're men in Grand Fenwick, not dogs. We don't live on handouts from the high tables of finance. We live on what we earn with the strength of our arms and the good of our soil. And while we keep it that way there will always be a Grand Fenwick whatever happens elsewhere. And while there is a Grand Fenwick there is hope for the world and for the rest of humanity."

All in all, it was one of the best speeches Bentner ever made. It brought another storm of applause in which Mountjoy could now heartily join. But Bentner wasn't through.

"You're going to ask me what we should do with this money," he said. "And you have got a right to ask. And I have got an answer. I've been thinking about it many a night. We'll do exactly what the United States does—we'll bury it in the ground. We'll sell out all those shares that we don't want and then we'll collect all those dollars that we don't want, and we'll put them in bales in the bottom of this castle and go on with our work like we did before."

This suggestion, after a very hot debate, was put in the form of a motion and voted upon. The motion succeeded, though not without meeting many perils. A counterproposal was made from the floor that all the shares be sold at a penny apiece. Mountjoy pointed out that to sell such vast holdings at a deflated value would seriously shake the American stock markets and might produce a recession in

Wall Street which would do enormous damage to innocent Capitalists.

"It is possible for Capitalists to be innocent," he added with an eye on Bentner. "Older people who have put their savings into stocks might be ruined overnight, and we have no right to inflict such an injustice on our fellow human beings," he said.

"The sudden sale of the shares is going to have a depressing effect on stocks anyway," someone said. But Mountjoy proposed that shares be disposed of privately if possible and without a panicky haste. He did not like the idea of bales of thousand-dollar bills lying about in the dungeon, either.

"That is altogether too dangerous," he said. "International thieves would undoubtedly endeavor to seize the money. I would suggest that the money be placed to our credit with a Swiss bank." But nobody would support that suggestion.

The sense of Grand Fenwick was that it wanted the dollars kept in bales in the dungeon of its own castle where the people could keep an eye on them. They could go in and look at them every now and then and it would give them a good feeling, said one member. Also it would be nice to have some ready cash handy in case of need.

Eventually Mountjoy, a glint in his eye, withdrew his opposition to that part of the motion, and the historic meeting closed with the decision to sell out and put the millions received in the dungeon of the castle.

Before the session recessed a motion was made from the floor expressing the gratitude of the nation for the efforts the Duchess had made to solve its unprecedented financial problems. The motion was passed by voice vote and the Duchess given three rousing cheers by the members.

"She's a genius," said one member. "We're very lucky to have her as our sovereign lady. Not many could lose four million dollars in four weeks and then make it all back plus hundreds of millions more."

"You know, there's something about women and money," said the other. "They just don't understand each other at all. Women think that money is what they want it to be and not what it is."

"Women think that everything is what they want it to be and not what it is," said the other. "And God bless them for it," he added fervently. "It's made a saint out of many a sinner."

CHAPTER XVII

The fact that Grand Fenwick was selling off its American investments and converting them into dollars was one of the best kept secrets of Wall Street and indeed of international financial circles. The sale was handled by Mountjoy, now appointed Finance Minister in what became a coalition government.

The world of finance knew only that Grand Fenwick was an immense investor in American stocks and that the wizardry of the ruler of the Duchy, Gloriana, was not matched even by the great Keynes. Even Ted Holleck believed in this wizardry and was astounded at how Gloriana had (as he saw it) foreseen every move he was about to make in the stock market and entered the ground quietly ahead of him. He contemplated flying to Grand Fenwick to meet her; contemplated approaching her on the subject of a joint cooperation which he was sure would make J. P. Morgan in the heyday of his activities look like the proprietor of a small-town dry-goods store. But in the end he decided that in such a partnership he might be outclassed. He was not a man to risk or endure being outclassed. And so instead of meeting Gloriana he resolved to avoid meeting her—to remain entirely apart from her and have no more communication with her in the future than he had had in the past.

Mountjoy himself journeyed to the United States to set in motion the liquidation of the Duchy's interests. So as not to attract attention to himself and his mission, he took a modest suite of rooms at a residential hotel (the Greystoke) off Fifth Avenue and brought with him, as his personal servant and bodyguard, Will Creman, whose only previous visit to New York had been as a member of the Grand Fenwick Expeditionary Force during its attack on the United States. He chose Will because he was a sentimentalist and he remembered that Will had met a girl called Rosie during his war service whom he had never forgotten. Will was delighted to go, and on their arrival in New York he showed Mountjoy the Empire State Building and said his plan had been to hold it to ransom as his personal booty of war.

"I think they'd have paid quite a bit to get it back again," he said. "But then, as Your Lordship says, money isn't really worth anything."

"I don't quite say that, Will," said Mountjoy. "But it is worth bearing in mind that money is most valuable when there is little of it and least valuable when it is available in quantity."

"They wear their dresses pretty short over here," said Will, who still had the eye of a soldier. "Long-stemmed American beauties. And good luck to 'em, says I."

Installed at the Greystoke, Mountjoy, following that procedure of delay which he believed the first essential of diplomacy, first did a little shopping on Fifth Avenue and obtained seats for himself and Will at the ballet and seats at the new home of the Philharmonic where he luxuriated in Haydn's "Oxford" and roundly denounced an offering of Tansman and another of Falla.

He spent an afternoon riding around Central Park in one of the landaus and could not resist visiting the Stock Exchange where, from the area reserved for visitors, he smiled down on the bustling, crowded floor, thinking what panic he could produce if anyone there recognized him and discovered the object of his mission.

Leaving the exchange, he dropped quite by chance into Hans's Bar, for he did not know of the place or its unique position in American finance. Hans, standing at the back bar as usual, did not know Mountjoy but recognized from his bearing that he was a man of importance and from his umbrella, tightly furled in contrast to his tie, which was rather loosely knotted, that he was a European. He served him a Pilsner lager; but these two great figures of finance met and parted without knowledge of each other, and the secret of the Duchy's decision to liquidate, which might have produced a panic, was preserved.

For the rest, Mountjoy called Mr. Balche and arranged for that gentleman to visit him in his rooms at the Greystoke. There he unfolded to the astounded financial agent the plans to liquidate all American holdings.

"This is to be done with complete secrecy," said Mountjoy. "Not a scrap of paper on the subject is to pass between us. Your instructions are to liquidate and there is attached to those instructions only this condition—not a word of what is going on is to be allowed out."

"And the price?" said Mr. Balche. "Surely you will want a floor?"

"Price is of no concern," said Mountjoy. "But the money realized is to be sent in actual American paper currency to Grand Fenwick."

"You mean in actual bank notes—not a transfer of credit?" said Balche.

"Yes," said Mountjoy. "I do not wish to be pressed here. You may use whatever machinery you wish, but the money must wind up in Grand Fenwick as actual paper currency. Not bonds. Not credits. Paper currency."

"Good heavens," said Balche, "this is without precedent. We'd have to use a fleet of armored cars to take the money to the airport. And I doubt that there are in Europe, outside of Army payrolls, one thousand million American dollars as dollars. However are we to get the money to you? We can't send bales of thousand-dollar notes through the mail."

"You are not a student of history, Mr. Balche?" said Mountjoy.

"To some limited extent," said Balche. "But what have you in mind?"

"The sending of great riches through the mail—third class—is not without precedent, you know," said the Count. "When the Transvaal decided to send the Cullinan diamond to the British royal family as a gift—a diamond, mind you, as big as a man's clenched fist—Scotland Yard was consulted as to how this could best be done without jewel thieves immediately seizing it. They advised sending two packages of about the same size from the post office at Johannesburg. One was to be heavily insured and go by first-class mail. The other was to be carelessly wrapped and sent by the lowest rate. The heavily insured package disappeared within an hour of being mailed. The other, actually a cigarette tin containing the diamond and sent third class, safely reached England.

"No, my good fellow, send us the money, not in a military plane or by diplomatic pouch, but in plain brown parcels bound with string and looking as though they contained old magazines. I will guarantee that every one of them will arrive safely."

"Are you really prepared to take such a risk?" asked Balche. "I assure you," said Mountjoy, "that if they were all stolen, not a soul in Grand Fenwick would turn a hair."

That evening, his mission completed, Mountjoy decided that instead of dining at Sardi's or Twenty-One or one of the other more fashionable restaurants, he would like to try a typical American menu. He mentioned this to Will, who said, "What we ought to do, my lord, is go to Times Square and have a couple of hot dogs at a stand they have there called Nedick's. Real good hot dogs, they are, with four kinds of relish. I've been thinking of one of them for fifteen years."

"You were at this place before?" said the Count.

"Yes, my lord. That's where I met Rosie. She thought I was a man from Mars in chain mail, but I told her not to be scared and she fixed me some coffee and one of them hot dogs."

"I doubt she'll still be there," said Mountjoy.

"Wouldn't like to come this far and not find out," said Will, blushing to the roots of his hair.

"Quite right," said Mountjoy. "'Hope springs eternal in the human breast/Man never is, but always to be blest...' You don't know Pope, I suppose."

"Born and raised a Baptist and I'll die that way," said Will doggedly.

They were disappointed when they got to Nedick's hot-dog stand in Times Square. A rather pimply young man with a paper cap served them their hot dogs. He was very busy and a trifle snappish; and when Will asked what had become of Rosie, he said he didn't know any Rosie and he had been there five years. Even Mountjoy felt saddened.

They stayed around awhile, but after half an hour it began to appear that they should leave, for others were waiting for their stools. They rose to go and Will found, standing behind him, a plumpish, good-looking woman, of middle years, reading a fashion magazine and holding the hand of a small boy. Mountjoy, in getting off his stool, jostled her and said, "I beg your pardon, madam."

Something in the way she turned her head set Will's heart beating faster. "Rosie," he cried.

She stared at him and said, "The man from Mars—I can't believe it. I've been coming back here ever since..."

They stared at each other and Will glanced at the child.

Rosie blushed. "It's my sister's," she said and then blurted out, "I'm not married."

"I think I'll go for a little stroll, Will," Mountjoy said. "That hot dog will take a little digesting. See you back at the hotel."

"Yes, milord," said Will. "Shall we be leaving soon—I mean for Grand Fenwick?"

"I will," replied the Count. "But I fancy it could be arranged for you to stay on a day or two if you have any personal—ahem—business to attend to. Good evening, miss." He raised his hat to Rosie and was soon lost in the crowd.

"Who is he?" asked Rosie. "Looks a bit like that feller that sells southern fried chicken."

"That's the Count of Mountjoy—the cleverest man in the world," said Will happily.

Mountjoy returned to Grand Fenwick a day later, his mission completed. Balche was to start offering the Grand Fenwick holdings on all the stock exchanges in the country, using whatever agencies and devices he thought would best preserve the secret of their ownership. The stocks found a ready market. Such an enormous number of shares, however offered, tended to depress prices, and to combat this Holleck and his syndicate started buying. The total holdings of Grand Fenwick were liquidated in three weeks, and shortly thereafter Mr. Balche faced the task of turning the billion-dollar bank credit of Grand Fenwick into actual dollars.

It was here that he met with an almost insoluble problem, which Mountjoy had quite casually dismissed. The Count had airily told him to just send the money in bales wrapped in ordinary paper. But the fact remained that no one bank had such an amount of currency in its vaults, and the request that it obtain that amount of currency from the Treasury or whatever was the proper source of supply would immediately start inquiries which would destroy the secrecy of the whole arrangement.

Balche had, of course, not made the deposit in one bank. He had deposited a million dollars in each of one thousand banks and he had been hard put to find a thousand banks to make the deposit in.

He could now go to each bank in turn and demand a million dollars in currency—a very large withdrawal in cash which would certainly lead to questions. Or he could subdivide the deposits still further until he had, say, one thousand dollars deposited in one million banks and branches of banks throughout the nation.

Mr. Balche wasn't quite sure that there were one million banks or branches of banks throughout the United States. But even if there were, he realized, after a little thought, that to put one thousand dollars in one million banks would be to complicate the problem enormously. Visiting ten banks a day and cashing a check for one thousand dollars in each of them would take him something over three years to collect all the money—allowing for weekends and holidays. And he was by no means ready to spend three years standing at cashier's desks in banks from Nome to New Orleans, cashing checks for a thousand dollars one after another.

Even with the deposit as it was—one million dollars in one thousand banks—it would require about five months of hard work at the rate of ten banks a day to send the whole deposit in cash to Grand Fenwick. And no banker was going to give him one million dollars in currency in five minutes. He would probably take a day or a day and a half and insist that the money be conveyed to its destination in an armored car.

So what was he to do? He decided that he must notify each of the banks in advance of the withdrawal, ensure that they had the currency available, and set up an appointment when he would be there with his check and his credentials to receive the money. He would ask for the currency to be made available in the largest possible bills, and wondered whether there was such a thing as a thousand-dollar bank note.

He found that this scheme worked reasonably well. He sent the letters to the bankers by registered mail marked confidential. He stressed in each letter that no word of the withdrawal of the deposit was to be allowed to leak out. In this he actually had the aid of the bankers themselves who were by no means ready to let others know that a depositor had withdrawn a million dollars in cash.

Gradually, but at an increasing pace, the cash began to collect. Mr. Balche picked it up in suitcases and to save travel, whenever a suitcase was full, sent it back to his New Jersey office by air express, having informed his staff to expect its arrival and to put it in his own office when it came.

He borrowed a page from Mountjoy's book and did not insure any of the suitcases except to the extent demanded by the air express company. Some of them contained as much as four and five million dollars in currency, and after rounding up a grand total of something over a hundred million dollars in this manner, Mr. Balche returned to New Jersey to find his office strewn with suitcases somewhere among which were his own clothes, sent in error.

He stayed behind when his staff left on the day of his return; and, having secured several large rolls of brown wrapping paper from a nearby five-and-ten, he started to bundle the currency up into suitable sizes which he wrapped in brown paper and secured with twine. He took these down to the post office on the following day only to receive the depressing news that he had to redo them because the clerk said they were the wrong shape. They could not exceed a total of forty-eight inches, adding the dimension of the four sides in one direction, nor a total of sixty inches adding the dimension of the four sides in the other direction. (Postal Regulations, United States, Government of, Parcels Section IV—VI subsection I, Paragraph 4, Overseas mail by surface only—Applicable to all countries but those abutting the Persian Gulf—See Notes Near East, pages 1196-1198.)

The next day he brought them back and this time got them off by surface mail, having convinced the clerk that Grand Fenwick did not abut on the Persian Gulf. The value he gave was nil. He stated that the contents were printed matter and took out no insurance.

"Old magazines, eh?" said the clerk. "You could send them cheaper just by bundling them up with the ends open." He glanced at the address. "Count of Mountjoy," he said. "Must be quite a reader."

"They're old comics," said Mr. Balche. "He likes Batman." All might have gone well, and complete secrecy been preserved and financial disaster on Wall Street avoided, but for Salat, the French bus driver. He was angry because, although Paris had at last been selected as the site of the peace conference between the United States and Northern Afghanistan, he had read that the Afghanistan delegates insisted upon being supplied with live goats and sheep, which were to be slaughtered, butchered and cooked in their own fashion.

"*Cochons*," he cried. "Pigs. French food is not good enough for these animals." He brooded over the studied insult to the great cooking of France by these barbaric foreigners. His temper was further inflamed by having to take up half his bus with a mass of tatty-looking paper parcels, much the worse for wear, addressed to the Duchy of Grand Fenwick, a foreign country, which he, a Frenchman, was obliged to serve.

All the way to the Grand Fenwick border he discoursed to his passengers on the shortcomings of foreigners when viewed from the French point of view. And when he pulled up at the guard post at Grand Fenwick he seized the parcels and started to fling them contemptuously into the road.

"For you," he shouted at the guard. "Tell them not to send any more. I refuse to have my bus littered with this trash." The parcels had taken much abuse on their journey so far, but this final tossing around by Salat proved too much for the string with which they were bound. Two of them burst open and spewed across the road a cascade of thousand-dollar bills.

All examined these in amazement and silence, broken at length by Salat. "Great heavens," he cried, his eyes bulging. "Money!" In a moment he and every passenger aboard were scrabbling in the road for the bills. They got a few, but the border guards retrieved them together with the broken parcels and the rest of the loose notes. Salat went roaring off, bursting with news of a vast treasure in American currency which he had delivered to the Duchy of Grand Fenwick, and so the secret was out.

CHAPTER XVIII

The news that Grand Fenwick had sold out its vast holdings in American stocks and had insisted upon payment in currency reached the world then as a result of the bad temper of a French bus driver. The shock to the stock market was immense. It dropped an average of three points within an hour of the report reaching Wall Street—transmitted by wire service from France, where it first appeared in an evening newspaper in Marseilles. The market continued down.

Many, before the Grand Fenwick story broke, had held that the market was too high and was due for a decline. That so great a financial wizard as the Duchess Gloriana should have sold out now confirmed that view and that she should have sold everything added a tinge of panic.

There was a rush to sell and that rush brought prices tumbling and panicked others. Perhaps some stability might have been restored and the panic stopped if there had been big buyers standing by ready to pick up the shares which were now being dumped. But the big buyers—Holleck notable among them—and the various mutual investment funds had already loaded up when Grand Fenwick was selling and they were already cautious.

Holleck held his holdings, but the mutual funds first refused to buy and then themselves started unloading shares in the hope of saving at least a margin of profit for their clients. Down the market tumbled further, in a cataract that was not to be checked by reason. Statements by bankers, by financiers, by respected members of the government, given on television and through the press, that the nation was solid and stocks were not overvalued, failed even to slow the deluge of selling. Finally, on the pretext that so much selling had taken place that the records were now hopelessly out of date, the New York Stock Exchange was closed for a week and other exchanges throughout the nation followed suit gratefully.

But during that week another terrible rumor got about. This was to the effect that Grand Fenwick intended to demand payment in gold for its dollar holdings. At the rate of $35 an ounce, the Grand Fenwick holdings in American currency amounted to close to a thousand tons of gold, give or take a couple of hundred tons.

A thousand tons of gold, it was said, was being readied at Fort Knox for shipment to the Duchy of Grand Fenwick. Every army truck seen in the vicinity of the famous Kentucky fort was rumored to be part of the convoy building up to take the gold shipment, which would require at least ten trucks to carry, to the port of departure. There, so the story went, a freighter whose crew would be heavily salted with G-men waited to convey the gold to Europe for eventual transmission to Grand Fenwick, where it was to rest in the dungeon of the castle.

Why was Grand Fenwick demanding gold instead of paper currency? The answer to that was simple. Because the Duchy, with its deep financial insight, had decided that the United States was about to devalue the price of gold in order to bolster its flagging paper currency. Rumors of such changes in the price of gold had been current for months, particularly after the United States had set its paper currency free of any metallic base in its domestic use.

The prospect that the same move might be followed in its overseas trading—that the nation might repudiate the gold basis of its currency in the hands of other nations—had haunted international financiers for months. So, when Grand Fenwick was rumored to be importing gold, others with American dollar credits began to follow suit. They were not, of course, following suit in actual fact, for the Duchy had no intention whatever of demanding gold for its bales of dollars. Those intentions had been imputed to the Duchy and reason amply supplied together with the details already touched upon. But the demand of other nations for gold in return for their dollar holdings was real.

France started to liquidate her credits and Western Germany also. Britain held out for a while, but facing a financial crisis of her own, and fearing the devaluation of gold, she also started to demand payment in bullion. And so from all quarters of the world there poured in a demand for American gold and the rumor went about (it was quite false) that there was not enough gold in Fort Knox or other lesser known U.S. depositories to meet the need.

There was but one exception to the general clamor. In the middle of the crisis *The New York Times* produced this cheery headline:

FINLAND OFFERS LOAN TO U.S.

In all this turmoil denial was useless. Those very media of mass communication which can plant a rumor in millions of minds simultaneously found that in trying to deny that rumor they were met with general disbelief. What was to be expected? people asked each other. Certainly the government would deny that it was shipping one thousand tons of American gold to the Duchy of Grand Fenwick. What government would openly admit to doing such a thing and hope to win the next election? It wasn't just ordinary gold either. It was American gold, and it evolved that the American people prided themselves very much on the American gold in Fort Knox, which gave them a sense of comfort—as Mountjoy expected the dollar bills in the dungeon of the castle of Grand Fenwick would give his people a sense of comfort too. The mass of Americans might never see the gold or touch it, but the fact that it was there was reassuring and the thought that it soon might not be there—that Fort Knox might become an empty box—was deeply disturbing. People got a sense that they and their ancestors had worked for centuries and now had lost everything. They felt that in a world where belief in God was weakening there had always been the dollar. And now the dollar was going because it was, after all, just a piece of paper.

The Cabinet of the United States, often in session on many matters, has rarely been called upon to consider the nature of money—something which was left to the Treasury Department and the members of the banking and securities commissions. But a full-dress Cabinet meeting was now called to consider the very real crisis which faced the country, unwittingly touched off by Grand Fenwick's disputed attempts to avoid wealth. In the course of that meeting the Secretary of the Treasury, Eben Roberts, son of a coal miner from the Pennsylvania pits, gave the President and the members of his Cabinet a discourse on the mystique of money which closely paralleled that given by the Count of Mountjoy to the Privy Council of Grand Fenwick.

"In essence," Roberts said, "money is an act of faith. It is not gold, silver, diamonds, or gourds (once used in the Republic of Haiti). It is nothing more than belief. What we are suffering from is a crisis of faith—a mounting of public doubt, national and international, to such a degree that faith in our money is going and may soon be gone. What we have to do is to restore that faith."

"Wouldn't the easiest way to restore faith be just to keep shipping gold to whoever asks for it and is entitled to it?" asked the Secretary of the Interior. "There will surely come a time when the whole thing will taper off, when the price of gold abroad will drop below the thirty-five dollars an ounce we ourselves have fixed. Then the gold will start coming back to us."

"We may run out of gold ourselves before that time comes,"

said Roberts. "The government has long realized that faith, not gold, is what supports our currency and we have allowed our gold reserve to become depleted as a result of demands over the years and our refusal to pay more than thirty-five dollars an ounce for the metal."

"Well," said the Secretary of the Interior, "we've got gold mines closed all over the United States. Let's open them up and mine ourselves a few thousand tons more."

Mr. Roberts smiled gently. "It costs about forty dollars to mine, crush and refine every ounce of gold we can produce here," he said. "We would be losing about five dollars an ounce—a big sum when you start talking in hundreds of tons."

"Why not raise the price of gold?" asked the Secretary of Commerce.

"Because to do so would be to devalue our paper currency," replied Roberts. "Right now, thirty-five dollars in paper will theoretically buy an ounce of gold. If we put the price up to forty dollars, then the paper currency is worth less and we have, in effect, cheated all our customers abroad who have dollar credits. More than that—loans we have made to other nations would have to be increased because they would have become devalued."

Something very close to a groan went up from the various members of the Cabinet. They felt themselves trapped. They were getting into an area which some felt was very close to magic and they felt incompetent to deal with the intangibles with which they were surrounded.

"Whatever did we do to Grand Fenwick that they should do

this to us?" demanded one.

"There is a misunderstanding about Grand Fenwick which I see is present even in this Cabinet meeting," said the Secretary. "Grand Fenwick had no intention whatever of visiting financial disaster upon the United States. I have been in direct communication with Her Grace, Duchess Gloriana the Twelfth, and with her Minister of Finance, the Count of Mountjoy. The fact of the matter is, astounding as it may appear, that Grand Fenwick was not trying to wreck our economy but was trying to avoid getting rich. The Duchy had no other ambition or aim than to remain in the economic situation which has served its people so well in the past. It found riches thrust upon it and it very sensibly resisted them."

The explanation of the whole situation, thoroughly documented, took two hours. It left the whole Cabinet silent and chastened.

"You know," said the Secretary of Commerce, breaking the silence that followed and speaking in a shaky voice, "we've got to preserve that country. That may be the last completely sane nation left on the face of the earth."

"Well," said the President, who had heard the story for the first time, "what are your recommendations? What do we do?"

"Through our embassy in France—we have, of course, not got an ambassador in Grand Fenwick—I have discussed this whole matter with both the Duchess and the Count of Mountjoy," said the Secretary. "The solution they offer appeals to me, though I do not understand it all, and I recommend that it be adopted, for I can think of nothing else.

"They ask that the treaty of peace between Grand Fenwick and the United States be amended to relieve them of the necessity of operating that chewing gum factory over here. They won't want any more profits."

The President swallowed hard. "Go on," he said in the silence that greeted the statement.

"They want the rest of their money, in dollars, sent to them, but they are prepared to pledge their national honor that they will not attempt to turn any part of it into gold.

"In return, the Duchess Gloriana will hold an international press conference at which she will assert her complete faith in the finances of the United States, the government of the United States, and the future of American industry and the capitalist system. She will say that she withdrew from the stock market here because she concluded that it was lacking in ethics for a nation as such to be a heavy investor in the stocks of another country, since nations should not compete against private individuals. She will further state that her country has greater faith in American paper currency, related to American production and marketing, than in gold, which has nothing but a romantic value and is not even a rare metal. And in proof of this, she will show the assembled press the bundles of American bank notes in the dungeon of the castle of Grand Fenwick."

There was a long pause while everyone considered this. "That sounds so wacky to me," said the President at last, "that, coming from the Duchy of Grand Fenwick, I believe it will work. Certainly it costs us nothing. So let's send them the rest of their money, revise the treaty and see what happens."

CHAPTER XIX

The international press conference in Grand Fenwick, designed to restore world faith in the finance and industry of the United States, was a vast success. Every variety of communications representative was there—newspaper, radio, magazine and television. The conference was held in the dungeon, where Gloriana sat prettily in a gold lame dress (a touch suggested by Mountjoy and frowned upon by Bentner) surrounded by stack after stack of American bills. The presence of so much money, mounting in tiers on every side, had a subduing effect upon the newsmen and the few selected financial experts who were present—among them Eben Roberts, Secretary of the U.S. Treasury.

It was he who handed to Gloriana from her hoard a sheaf of thousand-dollar bills so she could display them before the camera and say that these represented an investment in faith in the industry of the strongest nation of the world, and that was good enough for Grand Fenwick. Gold the Duchy did not require. The nation was quite happy to have its American credits in the form of bills.

"Whatever others may say," said Gloriana in concluding, "we in Grand Fenwick have complete faith in the United States and its people." That concluding statement brought a little flutter of applause from those present, and after a few words from Mountjoy and a few more from Bentner, who said that the riches of nations lay in the goods they produced and that the grape harvest that year would be of the usual superior quality, the interview closed.

Mountjoy was the last to leave the dungeon, taking a final look around before, as Minister of Finance, he pulled the heavy iron-studded door shut. Before pulling the door shut he turned to Roberts, the American Secretary of the Treasury, who had remained behind with him. "Do you happen to have a match?" Mountjoy asked.

"Certainly," said the Secretary and produced a box.

The Count lit the whole box and flung it into the dungeon among the stacks of currency.

"That makes you a gift of a billion dollars," he said. "I trust you will remember it in our favor."

"Such an act," said the Secretary piously, "will never be forgotten."

They shook hands and mounted the steps together, followed by a few wisps of smoke coming from beneath the dungeon door.

All then was resolved at last. The economy of the Duchy of Grand Fenwick was saved and so also, almost a by-product, was the economy of the United States of America. The world returned to its usual round of crises—a peace conference here, a threat of war there, a nuclear explosion in one place and a rocket launched to the planets in another. There was nothing now to disturb the Duchess Gloriana, or to occupy the busy mind of the Count of Mountjoy, who, to relieve his tedium, had set himself the task of solving the *Times* crossword puzzle daily without the use of any reference books, including dictionaries.

A month after the last of the financial crisis, when all had settled down, Mountjoy recalled that Dr. Kokintz had ordered some curious equipment some months earlier and went down to the great physicist's laboratory to see how things were with him.

The equipment he found in place and Kokintz gave him a very obscure explanation of its use, which, as far as Mountjoy could understand, started with canaries and wound up with linking sound and light together.

"You have heard, of course, of the speed of light and the speed of sound," said Kokintz, "the speed of light being an absolute by our methods of measure and the speed of sound varying according to the medium through which it is transmitted. Well, I have found that it is possible to accelerate the speed of sound and in effect to produce a sound which will travel faster than sound—to use a layman's concept. I have found that sound can be accelerated to very close the speed of light and that sound can then be transformed into light and thus from one kind of energy to another."

"Quite," said Mountjoy, who was beginning to regret the visit. "I hope that will have no effect on the immortal scores of Mozart," he added.

"Oh no," said Kokintz. "Who would want to tamper with Mozart? But it has some interesting possibilities."

"Such as?" asked Mountjoy.

"Well, look at that," said Kokintz, pointing. Mountjoy looked. What he saw was the brick from the castle wall which Kokintz had been using for a plant press. Only it was a dull yellow in color.

"You painted it?" asked Mountjoy.

"No," said Kokintz, "it's solid gold except for a small area in the center where the vibrations were..."

Mountjoy didn't wait for the rest. He reached for the brick and found it so heavy that he nearly dropped it.

"Solid gold?" he cried. "You mean you turned that stone to gold?"

"Yes," said Kokintz. "It was a matter of interfering with the nuclear orbits so as to produce an entirely different arrangement of the nucleus..."

"You can do that to anything?" asked Mountjoy, cutting him off.

"Just granite so far," said Kokintz humbly. "But with a big enough apparatus I could turn this whole castle into gold. But then, what would be the use of that? Who would want a solid gold castle?"

Mountjoy's head was in a whirl. Without going into details he saw immediately that Kokintz, able to mass-produce gold from granite, had stumbled on a device which could utterly ruin world finances. If gold, mass-produced, was worth no more than a few cents a ton, nation after nation would be ruined.

"Doctor," he said, "not a word of this discovery of yours must even be hinted at outside this room. While you have been busy here, we have just saved the Duchy and the United States from financial chaos. Now your discovery could undo everything and produce utter disaster and ruin in every nation of the world. You must dismantle your apparatus and discontinue your whole line of investigation."

Kokintz took his big Oompaul pipe from his pocket, filled it with tobacco, lit it and took a few puffs. "I will do that on condition of one promise," he said.

"What is it?" asked Mountjoy.

"Next time you want to burn a lot of paper in the dungeon please tell me. My birds suffered very badly from the smoke. They were very sick."

"I promise," said Mountjoy.

Kokintz nodded and, taking a can of dark-gray paint, proceeded to daub the gold brick with it thoroughly. "When it is dry I will put it back in the wall," he said. "It is too heavy now, in any case, to be of use to me, even for pressing my plants."

BOOKS IN THE GRAND FENWICK SERIES

Books 2 through 5 are best read after *The Mouse That Roared*, but all of the books can be read and enjoyed at any point in the series.

The Mouse That Roared (Book 1)

The Mouse On The Moon (Book 2)

The Mouse On Wall Street (Book 3)

The Mouse That Saved The West (Book 4)

Beware of The Mouse (A Prequel to *The Mouse That Roared*) *(Book 5)*

THE FATHER BREDDER MYSTERIES

Named "A Red Badge Novel of Suspense" alongside Agatha Christie, Michael Innes, and Hugh Pentecost, *The Father Bredder Mysteries*, written by Leonard Wibberley under the pen name Leonard Holton.

Father Joseph Bredder was a decorated sergeant in the U.S. Marine Corps. before becoming a Franciscan priest and amateur detective who both solves crimes and saves souls.

When Father Bredder gets involved with murder—Heaven only knows what will happen next…

"Amazing."
—LOS ANGELES HERALD EXPRESS

"Absorbing Mystery."
—LEWISTON JOURNAL

"Fast moving action … Father Bredder exercises his very special talents against extreme odds to solve a baffling mystery."
—HARTFORD COURANT

The Father Bredder Mystery Series

The Saint Maker
A Pact with Satan
Secret of the Doubting Saint
Deliver Us from Wolves
Flowers by Request
Out of the Depths
A Touch of Jonah
A Problem in Angels
The Mirror of Hell
The Devil to Play
A Corner of Paradise

ABOUT THE AUTHOR

Leonard Wibberley was born in Dublin Ireland, in 1915. He was the sixth child of a schoolteacher and an agricultural scientist. At nine, his family moved to London. Seven years later, when his father died, he went to work as a stockroom apprentice for a publisher and later became a reporter. After various jobs, he came to the United States in 1943 and engaged in newspaper work for ten years. While working for the Los Angeles Times, he published his first work, *The King's Beard*. Three years later, he published his most successful book, *The Mouse That Roared*, which was serialized in *The Saturday Evening Post*, and later made into a classic film starring Peter Sellers.

Wibberley lived in Hermosa Beach from 1949 until his death in 1983. With his wife Hazel, who clean typed his work, they raised six children and wrote over 100 books and hundreds of newspaper articles.

Check out his website at:

http://leonardwibberley.wix.com/author

Sign up for our monthly newsletter to receive columns written by Leonard Wibberley that were syndicated by newspapers nationally over his lifetime:

http://bit.ly/LeonardNews

You will also receive news of the upcoming releases of the ebook and paperback editions of his many novels, including his series of Father Bredder murder mysteries.

Made in the USA
San Bernardino, CA
15 June 2016